Strawberry Swirl Murder

A SPIES AND FOOD TRUCK COZY MYSTERY BOOK 1

ROSIE A. POINT

Strawberry Swirl Murder

A Spies and Food Trucks Cozy Mystery Book 1

Copyright © 2024 by Rosie A. Point

www.rosiepointbooks.com

All Rights Reserved. This publication or parts thereof may not be reproduced in any form, stored, distributed, or transmitted in any form—electronic, mechanical, photocopy, recording or otherwise—except in the case of brief quotations for review purposes.

This is a work of fiction. Any resemblance to actual persons alive or deceased, places, or events is coincidental.

You're invited!

Hi there, reader!

I'd like to formally invite you to join my awesome community of readers. We love to chat about cozy mysteries, cooking, and pets.

It's super fun because I get to share chapters from yet-to-be-released books, fun recipes, pictures, and do giveaways with the people who enjoy my stories the most.

So whether you're a new reader or you've been enjoying my stories for a while, you can catch up with other like-minded readers, and get lots of cool content by visiting my website at *www.rosiepointbooks.com* and signing up for my mailing list.

Or simply search for me on *www.bookbub.com* and follow me there.

I look forward to getting to know you better.

Let's get into the story!

Yours,
Rosie

One

"Who does she think she is?" The whisper was a vicious hiss that traveled in the salty air onboard the cruise ship.

It was a warm summer day, and I was halfway toward the kitchen on the VIP deck when the whispers reached me. I didn't react to them, partly because I had a boatload of ice cream to get into the walk-in freezers, but mostly out of habit. It was my job to keep my reactions neutral and to refrain from drawing attention to myself. A spy on the run should be seen not noticed, and that was exactly my aim this morning, and every morning for the foreseeable future.

"I heard she's on the run from her husband." That particular tidbit came from a woman with curly gray hair and round dark eyes. She reminded me of an owl.

"Did you? I heard that she's on the run from the police." Her friend, taller, hunched over, leaned in conspiratorially.

"The police? What for?"

The taller woman pursed her lips. "No idea."

I filed away the information for later dissection, another habit, and entered the cruise ships' kitchen. Compared to the cramped kitchen on board my I Scream for Ice Cream food truck, it was vast and shimmering with potential. Cooks moved through the space, calling out to one another, wearing their fancy white chef's jackets, busily preparing a delicious meal for the VIP guests.

And this wasn't even half of what they'd have to do today. Because tonight was the ship captain's birthday party—the reason I had been asked to cater with exotic ice cream flavors in the first place.

A young man in a chef's jacket that bore the cruise ship's logo—The Emerald Countess—stepped forward and smiled at me, showing off rows of white teeth. The smile was so bright and welcoming, it took effort for me not to recoil.

Relax. Not everyone's out to get you.

But it paid to be paranoid in my line of work. And my current goal was to keep my head down, keep my emotions in check, and not blow my cover *at all costs.*

"Hi," the chef said, brightly. "You must be the external contractor."

"April Waters," I said, extending a hand. Of course, April wasn't my real name. If I told this guy my real name, Delta Mission, I'd have to kill him. And I really didn't want to get blood on my shoes first thing in the morning.

That and he seemed friendly enough. And not suspicious at all.

You need to stop that.

"Jayce. You can store your ice cream tubs in the walk-in freezer." He gestured off to the left, where a silver slab of a door awaited me. "I'm the sous chef in the VIP kitchen. So, if you need anything, just holler."

He was young for a sous chef. "Thanks," I said, smiling.

"Come with me. We've cleared out some space for you," he said, and gestured for me to follow him past the rows of silver counters, past kitchen staff who were so busy, they didn't have time to glance our way. He opened the freezer door for me and held it. "Be careful with this one. It locks from the outside."

I scanned his face and kept my smile in place. "Creepy. Ever had anyone freeze to death in here?" I laughed as I tugged my trolley of ice cream tubs into the freezer.

Jayce's smile became fixed. "What? No. Definitely not. I haven't been here that long."

That was a really strange thing to say. But I couldn't and wouldn't trust easily, so there was that. "So how long *have* you been working here?" It didn't matter how long Jayce had been on board this ship, or why he seemed young for a sous chef, or why he was so jumpy about me mentioning death by walk-in freezer, but I couldn't help myself.

Part of the reason I'd become a spy was because I had this voyeuristic need to know people, to understand them, and to make friends. Because I was entirely sure that people would like me if I could be the type of person that was easy to like.

Jayce stood holding the freezer door open, watching as I unloaded the ice cream tubs. He cleared his throat and didn't answer my question.

I frowned and straightened, brushing off my blue jeans. "Sorry, did I pry? I've never been on board a cruise ship before, and I'm super excited. It's such a beautiful day."

"It is," he said, and his shoulders sagged. "The Emerald Countess is a perfect way to enjoy the ocean." He sounded like a brochure for the cruise line.

"I bet it is. It's a pity I can't stay on board."

"You're from the town?" Jayce didn't know where they'd put into port, it seemed.

"Carmel Springs?" I asked. "No, no. I travel the country on my food truck, so I'm new to town."

Jayce nodded. "All done?"

"Just about." I finished loading the last tub onto a clean polished metal rack, then exited the freezer, rubbing my arms.

Jayce gave me a sweet smile as he shut the freezer door behind me. "Just, uh, you let me know if you need anything else, all right, April?" He stepped forward, dropping his voice. "It's not every day we get a pretty girl like you in our kitchen, and I, uh, want you to be safe on board. Got it?"

"Why wouldn't I be?" I murmured.

Jayce's eyes shifted left and right. There was so much noise in the kitchen, the hiss of frying, clattering of pots and pans, people talking and clamoring back and forth, that he surely wasn't worried about who'd hear him.

The sous chef opened his mouth to say something then swallowed. "Just be careful." And then he skedaddled off, leaving a strange air of mystery in his wake.

Thankfully, strange airs of mystery were my forte. I exited the kitchen with my trolley and started across the deck. The cruise ship was a cream beast that sat in what I'd been told was the new cruise ship port in Carmel Springs, Maine —a tourist destination with loads of friendly inhabitants.

I couldn't wait to eat my fill of lobster rolls, to serve ice cream, and pretend that my life *wasn't* falling apart around my ears. Gosh, all I'd really wanted was to see more of my country, and now I got to do that. I shouldn't have been nervous or unhappy, but after recently losing my boyfriend—

"There she is!" The whispering continued from the two women who stood on the deck that overlooked the circular VIP pool. It was shimmering blue, and beside it was the VIP wavemaker. "See? The one in the kaftan. She really thinks she can just talk to people however she wants."

I scanned the deck below and spotted the topic of their gossip.

An older woman, her silvery hair lying in straight sheets against the sides of her face, wearing a colorful purple kaftan. She walked along, her nose in the air, pausing to prod at the deck chairs that lined the pool, or grimace at a towel that had been left hanging on the back of one.

"What is she doing?" the owlish woman asked.

"Probably checking whether everything is up to her standards. She's been on board for months."

A low whistle. "Where did she get the money?"

The kaftan-wearing woman scratched her leg then continued down the line of deck chairs. I studied her impassively as I passed by. She had a pattern, this woman. Walk a few steps, frown at the chairs, scratch her right leg. She did this action repetitively, almost like a tic.

I shook my head and left the gossipers to their complaints. I had a food truck to run, an event to cater, and an angry Iranian arms' dealer to hide from. In other words, my sundae was loaded up, with a cherry on top. I didn't have time to snoop or wonder why this woman was so hated, or why Jayce had acted so strange in the kitchen.

Especially when I mentioned murder...

<h1 style="text-align:center">Two</h1>

The party was in full swing, and I'd been set up behind the polished walnut bar, repurposed to become an ice cream serving station, for the ship captain's birthday celebration. The Emerald Countess had even provided me with extra wait staff to help man my ice cream bar, which was great.

Music pumped through speakers in the corners on the top deck, and the guests milled around or danced on the polished parquet square in front of the DJ booth off to my right.

In the distance, the view of Carmel Springs, its quaint port, the lights in the houses that encircled the bay, provided a scenic backdrop for the evening.

It would have been relaxing and enjoyable, except for the stress that the staff were under. The difference between the manic cooking and outright fear in the kitchen and the fun the guests were having was remarkable.

And it wasn't like I was imagining it. I made it my mission, last name pun intended, to trust my instincts.

"We're out of Strawberry Swirl." One of the waitresses, Tessa, scooped the last ball of it onto a sugar cone and handed it to a man with gray streaking his hair. He giggled like a gleeful boy and hurried off, licking his ice cream.

I loved that part of the job. Ice cream and joy went hand-in-hand.

"I'll get it," I said, and hurried toward the kitchen doors. They swung open, and I almost collided with Jayce on my way out.

He jumped at the sight of me, then put up a broad smile. "Nice to see you again, April. How are you holding up?" Jayce held a tub of ice cream in his tan hands.

"It's fun," I said. "I'm enjoying the party."

"I thought you might need a refill on the Strawberry Swirl. Seems like they're really enjoying that one."

"Thanks." I took it from him, and our fingertips brushed. "I'll have to run down to the truck and get extra if this carries on." I delivered the ice cream to the bar, and lost myself in serving customers.

They would arrive, sweating or irritable and leave again with broad smiles and ice cream cones clutched in their hands. A large portion of the customers were older folks, and for an ice cream party, there weren't that many kids around.

The ship captain himself was a strapping man in his immaculate suit, with a hat perched atop his salt and pepper hair. He'd already drawn a crowd of the VIP passengers, all of them hanging on his every word. Occasionally, a burst of laughter would float over from their group.

"He's not all he's cut out to be," Tessa said.

I glanced at her as she handed out an ice cream cone—Berry Ripple. "Sorry, what did you say?"

"The captain," she whispered. "He's not a good guy. Trust me. He's got plenty of secrets, and this front he puts up, that literally everyone buys into? It's all a game. If you get on the captain's bad side, you'll end up regretting it. But you didn't hear that from me." She pressed a finger to her lips. "Just be glad you don't work on this ship permanently, because it's full of secrets. Do yourself a favor and keep your head down."

"What do you—?"

A bark cut across my words, followed by a terrified shriek, and I snapped my head around, searching for the screamer.

"Get your horrible little thing off the VIP deck!" The shout came from a woman on the other side of the dance floor, closest to the silver railing that overlooked the pool deck.

Recognition sparked instantly. It was the kaftan-wearing woman the others had been gossiping about this afternoon. She squared her shoulders, straightening and sweeping back her silver hair, her eyes wide and fixated on the target of her disdain.

Another woman, her gray hair up in a messy bun, strands loose around her face, wearing a black pants suit with a bright orange fake flower pinned to her lapel.

A cream-colored pup ran back and forth on the deck between them, yapping its head off.

I liked all kinds of dogs, but even I had to admit, the barking was a little over the top.

"You leave Sir Barkington alone, Angela!" The suit wearer had an accent I couldn't place. Almost British? Australian? What was that?

Angela rearranged her kaftan and glared at the Chihuahua who ran circles around her feet. "You can't control this little creature, can you?" she asked. "You're as pathetic as it is."

"How can you talk about him like that? He's just a dog."

"She should know better. You should have trained it better, Hentie."

A fair point. And what kind of name was Hentie?

"Ja, well, you stay away from him. I know you tried to lure him into your cabin the other day, and you'd better watch it, because I'm not from this country, and I will kick you where the sun doesn't shine if you touch my dog." South African. The "ja" instead of "yeah" had given it away.

I'd been to the country once, for only a week, but it had been sunny, dangerous, and packed with interesting cultures.

"Who do you think you are, telling *me* what to do?" Angela asked, stepping toward her and raising a finger.

The argument had drawn a lot of attention. The ship captain, Quinton, adjusted the lapels of his uniform and started toward them.

"Don't you know who I am?" Angela asked. "You're lucky I don't have you and your dog dumped overboard." She stamped her foot, and the Chihuahua, Sir Barkington, yelped and made a run for it, darting off down the deck.

"Barkington!" Hentie cried. "Oh, no, Barkington. My poor dog, he's never been out of my sight before, he—"

A distant bark and yelp was followed by a splash.

I darted out from behind the counter and across the deck, dodging and weaving between the passengers. I hit the railing and looked around, spotting little Barkington in the kiddie pool on the deck below.

"No!" Hentie screamed. "He can't swim."

I darted down the ramp that led toward the pool deck, then vaulted over the railing and splashed into the kiddie pool, my jeans soaking through. Barkington dipped below the water, and I swept him into my arms and lifted him out of the water. He let out a soggy, choked bark and cuddled closer to my chest.

"You're fine," I said. "Don't you worry. You're fine."

The dog let out a whine then proceeded to shake itself dry in my arms, splattering my face and hair, and no doubt, smudging my makeup. I laughed and carried the dog back up to the party, where one of the wait staff held out a towel. I deposited the dog into it as a round of applause broke out.

I bobbed my head and smiled.

Two hands grasped my arms, and Hentie peered into my face, teary-eyed. "Oh, thank you. Thank you so much! You saved my poor little snuffy-wuffy Barkie face from drowning. You're the best person. You—" She broke down in tears and threw her arms around my neck, nearly strangling me in her joy.

Behind her back, Angela glared. And behind her, stood the captain, who stared at me with pursed lips and shaking his head.

So much for not drawing attention to myself.

Three

The commotion cleared up shortly after. Thankfully, it was only the lower half of my jeans, below the knee, that were wet. I squeezed them out as best I could, rolled them up, and dealt with it, resigning myself to a soggy night behind the bar serving ice cream.

Captain Quinton kept throwing glances my way for the next twenty minutes, his eyes narrowed, clearly displeased that I had taken the limelight at his party.

I kept myself busy serving ice cream cones and smiling at anyone who brought up my not so daring rescue of Sir Barkington—who had hastily retired, with Hentie, to a VIP cabin on board the ship.

"I told you, didn't I?" Tessa, the waitress whispered, ruffling her blonde bangs with a hand. She nodded toward the captain when he wasn't looking. "He doesn't like you one bit thanks to that."

"What should I have done? Let the dog drown?"

"Or waited for him to save the day," Tessa said.

"That's ridiculous. I should have held back to spare his feelings?"

She shrugged, her neat white uniform shirt rustling. "That's what he would've wanted. I told you he's not a good guy."

Good or not, he was none of my business. And the truth was, I shouldn't have sprang into action like that, simply because it might have given away that I had reflexes that were more honed than those of the other people on this ship.

But if saving a dog in danger was wrong, then I didn't want to be whatever the opposite of wrong was. I'd seen so much in the past few months that I wasn't sure what right was any more.

"We're almost out of Caramel Drip and Strawberry Swirl again," Tessa said, as she doled out yet another cone.

"I'll get it." I pulled on my sandals, dry after their brief stint in the water, and trudged into the kitchen.

The smells of cooking hit my senses, butter and lemon, seared fish, bacon. The scents were delicious, but I did my best to ignore them—I'd had a bite to eat at the Oceanside Guesthouse where I was staying in Carmel Springs before I boarded the cruise ship. I dodged past kitchen staff and irritable chefs, and headed for the freezer.

The door opened just as I reached it, and Jayce stepped out, carrying a tub of ice cream. Strawberry Swirl again. "Oh, hey," he said, with a charming smile that lifted one side of his mouth. "I thought you might need more."

I gave him a bright smile. "Thank you," I said, taking the tub. "But I need more Caramel Drip too."

"Let's hope none of the guests are lactose intolerant." He laughed and dipped back into the freezer. He reappeared with the second tub. "I'll help you carry it out."

"Thanks, but I've got it." I took the tub from him and stacked it on top of the Strawberry Swirl. "You don't seem too worried about someone locking you in the freezer after all."

His eyes widened incrementally, and then Jayce burst out laughing. "Right. That's funny. I was totally kidding about that before. I would never— I mean, there's never been anything like that on board the ship."

"Anything like what? Unexpected freezer deaths? Murder?"

Jayce's face paled a little, and he glanced off to the left. He forced a laugh, a bark of noise that traveled through the kitchen and drew the attention of nearby chefs. "That's— Yeah, nothing like that. I'd better get back to it."

"Sure," I said, lifting the tubs. "Thanks for these. But

how about you let me get them myself next time? Seems like you've got a lot on your plate."

"It's no trouble." And then he hurried off, moving between the silver stations, the cooking chefs. "We've got ten minutes until service. Ten minutes, so get everything plated and up to the pass."

I headed back through the kitchen and for the exit.

Jayce was hiding something—he didn't want me in the freezer, and he kept acting jumpy about it. Why? And why was he already ready with the ice cream we needed?

"Thank goodness," Tessa said, the minute I arrived at the bar. "I just had a passenger ask for two Caramel Drip cones." She took the top tub from me, set it down on the counter beneath the bar top, and popped off the lid.

I stowed the Strawberry Swirl in the freezer underneath the bar, thinking hard.

I'm not reading too much into this. Jayce was jumpy. The captain was strange. And Tessa had mentioned secrets on board the cruise ship.

None of which is your business.

The idea was to keep my nose clean. To make sure I didn't get any trouble, not dunk my nose smack dab in the middle of trouble. And I'd only just started my journey. The NSIB, the secret bureau I worked for, had flown me out here after the debacle at the Gossip Inn in Texas.

After I had lost... *everything* for the second time.

I needed a vacation from being me. I needed a vacation from stress and drama and gossip and worrying about who was after me or what people were thinking. So I would let this go. By this time tomorrow evening, the Emerald Countess would be on her way, fading into the lavender haze on the horizon.

"Excuse me! Pay attention, young woman." Angela, in her kaftan from earlier, stood in front of the bar, her sharp gaze fixed on me. "I've been trying to get an ice cream cone for the past two minutes. What kind of service is this? It's not what I expect on board a luxury cruise ship as a VIP passenger." She said the last part loudly and nearby heads turned to watch the fray.

Angela was the type of woman who liked to kick up a fuss and thrived on the attention that came from that.

"My apologies," I said. "Which flavor of ice cream would you like, Miss?"

"That's Mrs. Benson to you."

"Mrs. Benson," I said, correcting myself. "Which flavor for you this evening?"

"What do you have?"

"I have Caramel Drip, Chocolate Hazelnut, Berry Ripple, Chocolate Chip, Mint Freeze, Strawberry Swirl."

Angela held up a hand. "Strawberry Swirl."

"In a sugar cone or a cup?"

"A cup is fine."

"Of course." I opened the fresh tub of Strawberry Swirl and doled out a healthy helping into a cute cardboard bowl that was marked along the sides with my food truck's name.

"I Scream for Ice Cream? What a ridiculous name." Angela arched her eyebrows at the logo along the side, then snatched a plastic spoon from me. She brushed the back of her hand across her forehead, grimacing, then dug her spoon into the ice cream.

Angela took one bite, then turned and moved off. Except she didn't get far.

Two steps exactly.

Before she keeled over forward and hit the deck face first, drawing screams from the passengers.

Four

Nothing ended a cruise ship birthday party like a corpse.

The cruise ship had officially been "grounded" until further notice. The ice cream remained untouched in the freezer, and the police had arrived and directed us all to the pool deck below. The partygoers were in states of shock, but I caught sight of the two gossips from earlier in the day standing nearby with their heads together.

"Serves her right, doesn't it, Betty?" the owlish one asked.

Betty, the taller of the duo, hunched over, clasping her friend by the arm. "But what if we're next on the menu."

"The menu? She's a victim of murder, Betty, dear, not an entree."

"You know what I mean, Calliope," Betty replied,

craning her neck and sweeping a wary gaze over the gathered VIP passengers. "It's a good thing we didn't eat any of that ice cream."

"Keep your voice down," Calliope said. "She's right over there."

I didn't have to look over at them to know they were staring at the side of my face. They weren't far off, and I'd been getting looks ever since Angela had fallen over. The first thing I'd done was scream and draw attention to what had happened—not because I'd been afraid, but because it was the appropriate response to witnessing a death. At least it was for a civilian.

I'd seen much worse than an accidental poisoning.

But I wasn't convinced that was the cause of Angela's death.

It was all too convenient.

She took a bite of the Strawberry Swirl and dropped dead after a step. There were few poisons that acted that fast, unless it was something new or under development. And if it was a new poison, there would be no reason for it to be on board this cruise ship, unless I was the intended target.

And if I had been the intended target, poisoning the ice cream would have been the worst possible way to murder me, given that I was serving it to everyone else.

I let the thoughts form and undo themselves, creating

shapes and connections, like red threads on a corkboard. In my mind, images appeared.

A snapshot of the scene on the ship pasted to the corkboard, and threads spread from it in every direction. A red thread connecting the image of Angela's death to another of her fighting with Hentie, poor little Barkington running circles around them on the deck. Another thread heading off toward a picture of Betty and Calliope, their heads bent together as they watched Angela in the morning light on the upper deck.

The final thread traveled from the scene to a snapshot of Jayce, the sous chef, shocked as he emerged from the freezer, the tub of ice cream in his hands.

I didn't need to close my eyes to see the images. Served me right for having an eidetic memory—I could remember information with ease, a curse and a blessing because it drove me crazy a lot of the time.

I inhaled through my nose, held my breath, then released it slowly and held it again.

Jayce.

Jayce had been acting shifty and brought the ice cream out to me twice. The first tub hadn't killed anyone. Was it possible he had poisoned the second?

A memory of me popping the tab on the tub came back. It had been sealed.

There were two potential meanings.

First, that Jayce or the ill-intentioned third party who was the killer had masterfully poisoned the ice cream tub, either through injecting it with a syringe, or through another nefarious method.

Or second, that the tub of ice cream hadn't been poisoned and that Angela had died either of natural causes or through another method.

The only way I could figure out what had happened was to talk to the police and find out the true cause of death.

Which was *none of my business.*

"I can't believe she's dead," Betty said.

"Are we sure it's true?" Calliope asked. "I mean, I wouldn't put it past her to rise from the dead out of the blue."

"What, like a zombie?"

Calliope made a noncommittal noise. "You just never know."

"What, whether people will become zombies or not?"

"Of course not, Betty. That's ridiculous," Calliope sighed. "I suppose I'll have to call her cousin now, and let her know what's happened."

"Tell her I'm sorry for her loss," Betty whispered.

Calliope snorted. "Come on, I was Angela's sister-in-law, and even I'm not sad she's gone. Her cousin won't be either. Or her husband. If Roger had been around to see this, he probably would have danced on her grave."

Pleasant women.

And Calliope was the victim's sister-in-law?

I added that snapshot of information to the corkboard, watching another thread form. This was none of my business, yes, but I toyed with the puzzle anyway. My mind refused to be idle most of the time. I practiced my breathing and tried to force it to quiet while I waited for the inevitable.

The inevitable arrived in the form of a detective, wearing a neat pair of tan slacks, a short-sleeved buttoned shirt, and a shaved head. He toyed with his lanyard as he approached me. "You're the woman who served the ice cream, correct?"

The gossip around me quieted.

"Yes, that's me," I said.

"May I talk to you for a second?"

"Sure can." I followed him over to the side and we sat on one of the benches that ringed the pool deck, with its inlaid circular lights.

He cleared his throat. "My name is Detective White," he said. "Detective Abraham White."

"Nice to meet you, Detective," I said. "But I'd have preferred the circumstances to be different."

"You and me both, Miss...?"

"Miss Waters," I said. "April Waters." This was trouble. If I couldn't convince this detective of my innocence, he'd do some digging, and while I was confident in the NSIB's ability to keep my identity safe, there had been incidents in the past.

"A pleasure." We shook on it. "Can you run me through what happened tonight?"

"The ice cream tub was sealed," I said.

"I— What?"

I smiled at the detective. "Sorry, my mind is racing at the moment," I said, to disarm him. "The woman who ordered the ice cream cone from me ordered the Strawberry Swirl flavor in a cup. The ice cream tub was sealed." And then I told him about Jayce giving it to me, and how I had popped the tab on the tub before scooping ice cream out and into the bowl.

The detective took ample notes, nodding as I talked. "You're sure it was sealed."

"Yes," I said. "Are you sure it was poisoning? Because this could have been natural causes or another form of—"

"We're not sure of anything at the moment," Detective White said, with a huff of breath. "Only that you aren't going to be leaving Carmel Springs any time soon."

I'd planned on staying for a few months before moving on to the next town. "That's fine. I just wanted to make sure you had the information you needed to—"

"Excuse me." An older gentleman with gray hair and broad shoulders stepped forward from the group of passengers. He was a handsome guy, a silver fox was the right phrase, and he wore a pair of tortoiseshell glasses that sat on the tip of his nose. "I couldn't help but overhear you talking. Do you mind if I interject?"

Detective White looked as flabbergasted as I felt.

Five

"I'M IN THE MIDDLE OF QUESTIONING A WITNESS," Detective White said. "So I do mind if you interject."

"Sorry," the handsome guy said, "but I overheard you talking about a toxicology report, and I wanted to offer my services if you're in a rush to figure out what's going on. My name is Doctor Briggs. I'm the cruise ship's doctor, and I'd love to help out."

"That won't be necessary, thanks," Detective White said, pulling a face.

"You're sure? It wouldn't be any trouble. I could happily—"

"I'm sure." Detective White's tone brooked no argument, and the doctor shrugged.

"Just trying to be of service. You know us doctors, in

the business of helping people." And then he backed off, but not without a few glances back at us.

He wasn't yet worthy of a thread in my mind, and I didn't add him to the mental corkboard yet.

"Is there anything else you need from me, Detective?" I asked.

White scratched his chin, the stubble rasping. He removed a slip of card from his pocket and handed it to me. "This is my cell phone number. Call me if you think of anything else. As of now, you're not free to leave Carmel Springs, and neither is this ship. I've got your number here," he said, tapping his notepad with the end of his pen, "and I'll be in touch if I need anything else."

I nodded. "Thank you, Detective. If you need me to open my food truck for you so you can test the ice cream inside, I can do that too. It's parked out near the boardwalk, overlooking the bay." Helping him clear my name would work in my favor. The more attention he paid to me, the worse this would get, so if I could get him off my back fast...

"That would be very helpful. What's that truck called?"

"I Scream for Ice Cream," I said.

"That's a real strange name to choose for a food truck, ma'am."

"Yeah," I said. "It's meant to be a pun." And I hadn't

chosen the name. I hadn't even thought I'd be on another ice cream truck so soon after the last one.

My last cover had been an ice cream truck named Gerry's Gelato, and I'd had to cut my hair short and color it bright red. Now, I had dark hair that was fast growing out into an unruly bob. I brushed my fingers through it, got up, and started toward the group of passengers waiting nearby.

Betty and Calliope glared at me, their arms linked. They'd opted for breezy dresses with sandals, and they looked like a much older version of those twin girls from *The Shining*. Except mismatched and more menacing.

I stood under a cabana poolside, my arms crossed, waiting as the detective drew yet another passenger aside to talk to them.

A murder or natural causes.

The woman had clearly been hated, but how had she been killed?

Not poisoning?

I practiced my breathing as the detective approached Betty and Calliope.

"Mrs. Calliope Benson?" Detective White asked. "Do you mind if I talk to you? I have some questions about your sister-in-law."

Calliope wet her lips and looked down at her friend

Betty, who gave her a nod, like she was permitting her friend to talk to the detective.

I was surprised the detective hadn't immediately rushed off to go talk to Jayce. The kitchen staff had been pulled out and were off to one side of the kiddies pool, gathered and talking. One of them had a cigarette in hand and gestured with it, occasionally sucking on the filter.

They weren't allowed near the VIP guests. I was only here because I wasn't in uniform, and because I was nosy enough not to care if they didn't want my presence.

"There you are." Hentie bustled over to me, grasping her dog, Barkington in her arms. He wore an orange and pink striped doggy sweater that matched the orange flower in Hentie's lapel. "I go to my bedroom for a couple of minutes and come back to this chaos. Wat op aarde gaan aan?"

"I— What?"

"Sorry," she said. "Habit. I said, what on earth is going on?" Barkington barked, and she shushed and kissed him on the head. "Voei tog, Bluffy."

I was intrigued by the language she was speaking, Afrikaans if my memory served, but she'd asked me a question, and I was keen to witness her response to the news, because she'd been fighting with Angela shortly before her death.

"Angela died," I said.

Hentie choked on air. "W-What?"

"She died," I said. "Took a bite of ice cream and fell over."

"Well, you cut straight to the chase, don't you?" she asked.

I shrugged. "The police think it's a murder. They're grounding the ship."

"No," Hentie said. "But this is meant to be our holiday. Barkington and I are taking a break from Franklin. He's going to be worried if we don't come back on time."

"Franklin?"

"My husband," Hentie said. "He's an oil magnate in Texas. Very old. Liable to pass away at any moment, but a good man."

I acted appropriately intrigued.

"You think I'm weird, don't you?" Hentie asked. "That's fine, a lot of people do, and I can't say I care. Anyway, that's enough about me, let's talk about Angela. She's really dead?" The way she moved from one topic to the other was both disconcerting and refreshing.

Barkington's bark was more upbeat this time.

Hentie shushed him. "You should never wish ill on people, Bluffs."

"She's dead," I said. "Any idea who might have wanted to—"

"What... ice her? No idea," Hentie said, then hesitated.

"Now that you mention it, there are a few names that spring to mind. She wasn't the most popular person on board the ship. And she's been around for a long time, irritating everyone."

"I heard about that," I said. "That she's been here for a while."

"She's on permanent vacation. One of the lifers like me," Hentie said, pointing to her chest.

"Lifer?"

"Oh yeah. I spend all my time on the cruise ship. My husband is busy with work, and he likes to keep me entertained. I visit him twice a year for a month or so at a time, mostly over Christmas, and that's it. Otherwise, I'm free to explore as I wish. That's my story, but I don't know what the deal is, sorry, was, with Angela. She's been on board The Emerald Countess for months." Hentie sighed. "And it hasn't been easy. We've found it best to avoid her."

"She made people on board *that* uncomfortable?" I find it difficult to believe. Not impossible, just difficult. She'd been awful to me at the ice cream station.

"Ja. I'll say that if you can find one person on this ship who liked her, I'll be surprised." Hentie narrowed her hazel eyes to slits. "And if anybody tells you they liked her, well, those are the people I'd be suspicious of if I were you."

Which was an easy out for her, since she'd hated the

victim. Not that I blamed her after the way Angela had treated her dog.

I shouldn't have been invested in this, but with little else to fixate on except for ice cream and grief, my thoughts turned to the corkboard and who could have murdered Angela Benson. Assuming it *was* murder.

Six

I woke up the following morning, bright and early, on a comfortable cloud of pillows in the quaint Oceanside Guesthouse. Before coming to Carmel Springs, Maine, I'd spent a good amount of time researching where to stay, and this place was the best reviewed.

The guesthouse was situated right along the bay, with a back porch that led to a path onto the beach. The house itself was surrounded by beach scrub and had shiplap walls, and the cutest dining area where guests would gather at the polished round tables and chatter while waiting for their breakfasts.

So far, breakfasts at the Oceanside had been a great way to start my mornings. But this morning, I was obsessed with what had happened on the cruise ship last night.

I made quick work of preparing for the day, my reflection in the mirror over the sink pale, with dark circles under my eyes.

It wasn't like I'd ever slept well, what with being a spy and all, but that corkboard...

That corkboard...

I shut my eyes as I gave my hair a quick brush and went over it in my mind. The threads. The connections.

My eyelids fluttered open, and I finished dressing, then hurried out of my room.

"Will you be joining us for breakfast, April?" Sam, the owner of the guesthouse, called from the dining room.

I waved to her. "Not this morning, sorry, Sam."

"No problem!" She tucked strands of mousy brown hair behind her ears and retreated into the sunlit strewn dining room.

I rounded the front desk, hopped out of the path of the guesthouse cat's, Trouble, swatting calico paws on the way to the front door, and was off.

The cruise ship cut an ominous figure in the early morning light. It was just past eight, and already, there were people on deck. I'd already offered my truck keys to the cops last night, and Detective White had impounded it while they investigated. Annoying but necessary.

I darted up the gangplank, onto the cruise ship, and made a beeline for the VIP deck. Any time I spotted a staff member approaching, I turned down a different passageway.

I found my target exactly where I'd expected.

Calliope Benson stood near the party area from last night, overlooking the pool deck. She wore a floaty white dress, held a tote to her side, her head tilted toward the much shorter Betty, whose mouth was moving relentlessly.

When I'd overheard Betty and Calliope gossiping here yesterday morning, I'd presumed that this was their spot.

Most people were creatures of habit. They didn't find it necessary to vary what they did each day, and in doing so, they created obvious patterns of behavior. Ones that people who had a particular set of skills could use to their advantage.

"…terrible, but I don't think that anyone would disagree," Betty said.

Calliope opened her mouth, but spotted my approach and her eyelids fluttered. She went from standing tall, drawn to her full height, in full gossip mode, to hunched in the span of a heartbeat.

"Good morning," I said. "How are you today?"

"What are you doing here?" Betty asked. "Aren't you the one who poisoned—"

Calliope hissed at her friend to silence her.

"Just here cleaning up after last night," I said, with a

smile. "How are you doing? I know this must be very diffi-cult for you."

The wrinkles on Betty's brow grew more pronounced. "Why would this be diff—"

Another bout of shushing from Calliope. She dabbed at the tip of her nose, her mouth turned down at the corners. "Yes, thank you, this has been awful. Of course, my sister-in-law wasn't the easiest woman in the world to get along with, but she was family."

"But that's not what you said last night," Betty cut in.

Bless her heart, she was either slow on the uptake or being purposefully unhelpful to her friend's cause.

"Betty," Calliope snapped. "Can you please give me some space? I'm clearly going through something right now, and this lovely woman would like to talk to me about it."

"I thought you said she was suspicious." Betty wrig-gled her nose.

"Get out of here." Calliope's tone was deathly cold.

Betty took one look at Calliope's expression and scut-tled off.

"Sorry about her," Calliope said, turning to me, that sorrowful tone back. "She doesn't know when or how to keep her mouth shut, but she means well."

I've heard that about people who wish ill on others. "That's okay," I said. "You didn't have to ask her to leave. I just wanted to offer my condolences to you. I understand Angela was your sister-in-law."

"Yes," Calliope said, clutching the railing. "I recently joined her on board the cruise ship. I didn't expect us to get on well, honestly, because she's always been a difficult woman, but I have to say it was nice to have a family member on board."

"I'm sure that must be difficult for you, and now a murder investigation as well." I pulled a face. "Awful."

"We'll see how long that murder investigation lasts," Calliope murmured, her eyes glimmering. She swept her gaze to the pool deck below, the passengers, the towels that were neatly folded and stacked on the seat of each deck chair. "I have to say, I didn't expect my trip to go this way."

"Nobody expects this type of thing of a VIP cruise. Those tickets must have cost you a lot."

"Me?" Calliope laughed. "Oh no, not me. It was actually Angela who paid for them. She was loaded. An inheritance from my brother."

"Oh, I'm sorry for your loss," I said.

Calliope waved a hand, her tote bag shifting down her arm so she had to pull it into place again. "My brother was old. He was bound to pass on sooner or later, but we weren't particularly close. Still, I took it as my duty to come on board and spend time with Angela after his passing. It was the right thing to do."

"So he passed recently?" I asked.

Calliope stiffened, her knuckles whitening on the railing.

"Sorry," I said. "I shouldn't pry. I'm one of those people who loves to gossip. It's a curse." I gave a self-deprecatory laugh and shrugged.

"There's nothing wrong with a bit of harmless gossip," Calliope said, her eyes lighting up.

"That's what I always say." I pressed a hand to my chest. "What's the harm? It's not like it's going to hurt anybody."

Calliope nodded her head, fervently. "Yes, exactly. I can never understand people who take issue with it. It's just talking. Words are just words. Good heavens, everyone is so sensitive nowadays."

"I totally agree," I said. "I'm April by the way."

"Of course, the ice cream truck girl," Calliope said. "Lovely to meet you properly."

"And you," I said.

Calliope checked her watch. "Well, I should run. It's just about time for brunch. If you're around this evening, maybe you could join us for dinner and the show. They're going to have a comedian, a snake tamer, and an aerialist perform tonight."

"That would be amazing," I said. "I'd be thrilled to join you."

Calliope hurriedly withdrew a pen and a scrap of card from the tote bag on her shoulder and scribbled down the details, then foisted the card into my hand. "See you then!"

"Have a good day," I called.

A rustle of movement to my left, near the doors that led into the kitchen caught my attention. And I turned in time to spot a wide-eyed Hentie darting out of sight into the kitchen proper. A moment later, the silver doors, complete with porthole windows, swung open again as she was escorted out by one of the kitchen staff in chef's whites.

Barkington yapped in her arms. "Oh sorry," Hentie called. "I didn't mean to go in there. Jinne man, I thought it was the toilets." She met my gaze and gave me an uneasy smile.

"Hentie," I said. "Fancy running into you here."

Seven

"It's not what it looks like," Hentie said.

Barkington barked.

"What does it look like?" I asked, raising an eyebrow.

"Well, look, okay, it's exactly what it looks like, but I have a good reason for eavesdropping on your conversation," Hentie said. "I happened to know both Angela and Calliope very well, and I wanted to make sure that she wasn't lying to you."

"Why would it matter if she lied to me?"

"I don't know," Hentie said. "I just don't trust her. Look here, the thing is, Angela was my friend."

I frowned.

"I know, I know, I didn't exactly come out and say it last night."

"You told me to be suspicious of her friends. You acted

like you didn't know her, and you said she was an awful person."

"Not really. She was just difficult to talk to. And be friends with. But I did try. We were friends, even if it was a difficult friendship to have. I didn't like her, but I figured it's better to be on her side than on the opposite side to her because she was kind of evil. And look, I just didn't want people thinking bad of me because I knew her."

"So you were friends with the mean, evil woman so that you—"

"Ja. I didn't want to be on her wrong side, you know?" Hentie hurried toward me and stopped, holding my gaze. Today, she had opted to do her messy gray hair up in a high ponytail that fountained from her head, and she wore another pants suit, this one in beige, the shirt underneath covered in bright orange floral print. "Look, you don't understand what it's like to live on board one of these ships," she said. "The people here will chew you up and spit you out before you know it. The lifers? We're the ones who know all the ship's secrets. We're the ones in the most danger."

"Danger? What do you mean?"

"This ship is not as innocent as you think it is," Hentie said.

It was the second time she'd said something of the like.

Hentie gestured for me to follow her, and we walked

along the VIP deck together, past luxury cabin doors that were spaced far apart. She stopped in front of one and opened it with a shaking hand. Barkington gave a few barks and she set him down so he could rush inside.

"Listen," she said, "I'm only telling you this stuff because I know that I can trust you. Serial killers don't usually save little animals."

This was a common misconception. Many serial killers were sociopaths who knew how to manipulate public opinion by appearing to be giving and kind and caring when they weren't. They operated in the dark, under the guise of being something they weren't.

It made me uncomfortable to think about, especially since I operated under a similar guise as a spy. And I didn't like to think of myself as nasty and manipulative.

"Come in, come in."

I followed Hentie into the fabulous interior of her luxury cabin, but I kept the door open a crack. I wasn't afraid of her, but it was better to keep an escape route visible and accessible at all times.

"If this ship is not innocent, why are you still on board?" I asked.

"That's an excellent question," she said. "And the truth is, it's a luxury ship, and I only suspect there's nefarious stuff happening. It's not like I have the proof to back it up. Captain Quinton would never allow that."

"What do you mean?"

"He's in complete control of this ship. Not just as the captain but in every way. The lifers know to stay out of his way, and the passengers who are here temporarily, well, they don't know anything about it. This isn't the first death on board."

"There have been others?"

"Oh ja. There was one a couple of months ago, just after I boarded the ship," she says.

"It all happened so fast, and—"

Footsteps on the deck outside silenced Hentie, and I stepped behind the door, prepared to shut it, but a glimpse of the captain's smart white jacket stopped me.

"So, this will be dealt with appropriately," Captain Quinton said. "I won't have to deal with your officers darkening my deck?"

"We've got everything we need," Detective White said, his voice rasping and low. He sounded bone tired, and I froze, my palm flat against the back of the door.

Hentie had gone pale, and Barkington snuffled around at her feet. She swept him into her arms and placed a hand on his furry head, likely to stop him from barking.

"I won't bother you with this again," he said. "It looks like you're free to leave port in the next few days, assuming nothing else turns up."

"I trust that it won't," Captain Quinton replied.

"There's nothing to hide on board my cruise ship. It's very unfortunate that a passenger has passed on and in such a visceral manner, but you have your avenues to investigate now."

"Yes, well, we're still waiting for the initial toxicology report, but thanks to your input—"

"Yes, yes," Captain Quinton said. "If you'll excuse me, Detective, I have important matters to attend to."

"Of course."

Steps clattered on the deck, and then a throat was cleared. "Captain Quinton?" Detective White called.

"Yes?" The captain's voice was further off.

"When do you plan on leaving port?"

"About seven days," Quinton replied. "We have a few loose ends to tie off here before we leave. Restocking and so on. Why do you ask?"

"Just good information to have. Have a good day, sir."

"I trust that I will."

Finally, the footsteps retreated, and I released a breath, shutting the door quietly. I turned to Hentie. "Looks like you were right."

"I knew he was up to something," Hentie said. "Did you hear that? Business to attend to. And what was that about leaving Carmel Springs? How can the detective let him go? I'm not familiar with how things go in America, but can that detective let the whole crime scene float away?"

I pinched my chin and inhaled slowly, held it, then exhaled and held it again.

"What are we going to do about this?" Hentie asked, petting Barkington with renewed vigor. He whined and wagged is tail, cuddling closer to her.

I swept my gaze toward her. She was still a suspect, even if she was a good source of information. "Nothing," I said.

And then I swept out of her room, studying the corkboard in my mind. A thin red thread spread from the image of Angela's body, prone on the floor, to another snapshot, one of Captain Quinton glaring at me past her shoulder.

Something was *fishy* on The Emerald Countess, and it wasn't the lobster boats in the harbor.

Eight

That evening, I dressed in a flowery cotton dress, put on a splash of makeup, and headed out of the doors of the Oceanside Guesthouse, determined not to focus too much on the corkboard or my thoughts. Not because I didn't want to figure out what had happened to Angela, I did, but because staying trained on the present moment would help.

I found that my brain would fixate and torture me if I didn't force myself to connect with the real world once in a while.

It was a beautiful summer's night, the air crisp, the dusk falling in a haze over the sky, and my heart turned and squeezed in my chest. Tears pricked at the corners of my eyes as I took the pathway up to the VIP deck.

My ex-boyfriend's face swam into view in my mind,

captured in picture-perfect clarity. If I closed my eyes, I would be able to reach back in time, to a memory of him, before he'd died.

Instead, I met Calliope in front of the VIP dining hall.

She wore a set of glimmering diamond earrings and a broad white smile. "There you are, dear. I'm so glad you made it."

"I wouldn't miss this for the world," I said. "I don't get a lot of opportunities to go to fancy shows."

"Of course, of course." Calliope patted my arm. "You poor thing. You must not get out a lot. I'm sure that's difficult for you, being poor and all."

How out of touch can one person be? I had my judgemental side. "Yeah, this will be fun."

"That's a quaint dress," Calliope said, nodding to my summery cotton slip. "Rather understated for dinner, but you'll be fine. Come on inside." She offered my arm, and I linked with her as we entered the VIP dining hall.

A chandelier, laden with teardrop crystals, hung in the center of a room themed in golds and whites. It felt like I had walked into heaven, and the smells from the kitchen—the kitchen with the suspect freezer—certainly made it seem that way.

"Our table is right at the front. See the stage?" Calliope gestured to a chair.

I sat down with her, and Betty, who wore a string of pearls and a velvet dress, nodded to me, patting her gray hair. She cast a sidelong glance at Calliope, whose lips instantly thinned.

"Hello, uh…"

"April," I said.

"Really, Betty, you need to start paying more attention. I told you what her name was. She's the woman with the ice cream truck, remember?" Calliope's words were scathing, and Betty lowered her gaze to her half-empty glass of wine.

The dynamic intrigued me. Calliope and Betty had despised Angela, but Calliope wasn't acting any kinder than her sister-in-law.

"All the festivities will take place on stage."

The stage was low, made of polished wood and flanked by two cream curtains that were drawn back to show off two swathes of silk that dangled from high above and brushed the top of the stage.

"The aerialist will swing from those," Calliope said, leaning her pointy chin in her palm. "But first, the comedian, and the snake tamer. It's going to be an amazing— Oh! There you are, darling!"

Another woman, barefoot and wearing a pair of harem pants that swished as she walked, approached the table. She had on exotic shimmering green eye makeup that matched the tint of her lipstick. She had to be in her twenties, maybe early thirties, around my age.

"Calliope, my sweet Goddess of a friend," the woman said, and swept into a bow.

Calliope tittered. "Oh, you've always had a flair for the dramatic," she said, patting the other woman's arm. "What a treat to have you here to meet our new friend. April, this is the snake tamer, Eve."

"Nice to meet you," I said, shaking her hand. She had a firm grip, and even the tips of her nails were painted a venomous lime.

"Eve's just a stage name," she whispered, with a conspiratorial wink. "My real name is Becky. But Becky the snake tamer didn't have as much of a ring to it as Eve, if you catch my drift."

"It's lovely to see you again, Eve," Betty said, blinking those large eyes at her. "We had hoped we'd catch you at the Captain's birthday party."

"I couldn't make it unfortunately. I was feeling under the weather."

"Oh no," Calliope said. "Is everything all right?"

"All's well that ends well, as they say," Eve replied, with a smirk. "But let's just say my end wasn't feeling very well that night." She pointed at her bottom. "Thankfully, Doctor Briggs didn't mind being pulled away from the party for a couple of minutes to give me something to deal with the cramps."

"Oh no," Betty whispered. "Did you eat something bad? What if it was in the shellfish?"

"Goodness, Betty," Calliope said. "You and your anxiety. There are worse things a person could eat than bad shellfish."

"Bad shellfish can kill a person," Betty said.

"So can poisoned ice cream, I hear," Eve murmured, leaning one tan hand on the table. "I heard about Angela."

"It's not confirmed yet," Calliope said, leaning in to enjoy the gossip, even though she was gossiping about the death of her own sister-in-law. "We'll see what the police have to say."

I observed the interaction, but kept a concerned frown. "I hope you're okay, Calliope. I know this must be tough for you."

"Tough for her?" Eve barked a laugh. "The woman was a menace. Calliope couldn't stand her."

"Nobody could stand her," Calliope added in, hurriedly, and swept her fingers along her hairline, then rubbed her fingertips together. "Eve, darling, you simply must join us when you're done with the show tonight."

"You know what they say, Cally. No fraternizing with the guests. Captain Quinton will lose it if he sees me dining with you." She glanced around the room and pulled a face. "I'd better get out of here before he spots me." She winked at us then hurried off again.

"She's something isn't she?" Calliope asked. "A real super star."

"And a nasty gossip," Betty said. "She loves to talk about people behind their backs."

"Oh, Betty, please, keep your silly opinions to yourself. You're upsetting me, and I haven't even had the chance to have a sip of my wine yet."

The dinner was served in courses, and each course was accompanied by entertainment. It was fun, experiencing new foods and sights. The aerialist's act reminded me of a stint I'd done behind the scenes at the Cirque du Soleil, and the snake tamer, of Morocco, for some reason. Maybe because of the music she played along with it.

"Thank you so much for inviting me," I said to Calliope. "What an amazing evening."

"I love making new friends," she said. "You are so welcome, of course."

"And with all that money she's going to get from Angela's death, she sure can afford to treat you," Betty put in.

Calliope dropped her knife and fork with a clatter.

Nine

"Betty!" Calliope snapped the word out like a curse. "What are you talking about?"

"You told me that you're going to inherit everything from your brother now that she's gone, right? I'm sure you told me that." Betty tapped her finger against her glass, wide-eyed and innocent, like she had no idea what she'd done wrong.

But I was fairly certain that Betty knew exactly what she was up to. This felt like a *Mean Girls* coup.

"I have no idea what she means, sorry," Calliope said. "No idea. Just forget she said it."

I gave a polite smile. "Of course," I said. "It' none of my business. And besides, I heard today that the ship is going to leave port soon."

"You did?" Calliope asked, leaning forward, and that same excited shimmer took its place in her eyes. "You're sure about that?"

"Yeah, I overheard a conversation between the captain and the detective who is investigating the case. Maybe it wasn't a poisoning after all." But the way things had gone on this ship, I wasn't so sure. There were plenty of suspects, and there was something... Something on my corkboard, an image that was blurred, that hadn't revealed itself to me yet.

This was murder.

My mind was certain of it, but I hadn't found the correct puzzle pieces.

"We're leaving soon?" Betty sounded puzzled. "But she died. She just died."

"Betty," Calliope snapped. "You don't need to talk about my sister-in-law like that."

"Have *you* heard *you* talk about your sister-in-law before?"

She was funny, Betty, without even trying, and I liked that about her. I took a sip of my wine, I'd barely touched it, and watched the interaction between the women over the rim of my glass. Calliope wild-eyed and excited, Betty frowning.

I'd let slip what I'd overheard for exactly this reason. If

Calliope wanted to get away from Carmel Springs and out to sea, she had to have a reason for it.

The final course, dessert, was served, and a waiter dressed in more of that spotless white placed a plate in front of me, bearing a chocolate lava cake. I thanked him and glanced toward the porthole doors that led into the dining room.

A familiar face peered through one of them.

Jayce, the sous chef. His gaze collided with mine, his eyes widened, and he dipped out of sight.

Calliope wasn't the only one on board who had something to hide. Jayce did too.

I took a few bites of my lava cake, made the appropriate noises—it was divine, but I was more of a caramel girl rather than chocolate—and rose from the table. "Thank you so much, Calliope. This was amazing. I've never experienced anything like this before." A lie. I'd spent two weeks on my own in the Appalachian Mountains, training for a special ops mission, and had encountered *strange* things up there.

"You're leaving already?" Calliope asked, her words slurring a little. "But the evening has scarcely begun."

"I should get back to the guesthouse," I said. "I'm pretty beat, and it was a lovely evening."

"Sure. Well, come back again," Calliope said, not bothering to get up.

Betty smiled at me and waved, then picked up her glass again and leaned in to start a gossip session with her friend. Or frenemy, I wasn't sure how they defined it, given how they treated each other.

I walked out of the dining hall and into the salty air on the deck. And then I turned left and walked along it, toward the party area that overlooked the VIP pool deck. Another left brought me to the silver kitchen doors with their porthole windows.

I peered inside, sweeping my gaze over the kitchen. I kicked off my strappy shoes, picked them up and held them in my hand, the breeze brushing against the backs of my knees.

Where are you?

Jayce stood near the freezer in the back, pale, his eyes darting left and right. And then he started toward the exit where I stood.

I backed up and waited beneath one of the shell-shaped sconces.

The door swung open and Jayce emerged, looking directly ahead and fumbling a cigarette and a lighter out of his pocket.

"Do you usually smoke out here?" I asked.

He screeched, a wild terrified noise, and threw his lighter up. It turned end over end and clattered down on his head, then slid sideways onto the deck.

"Sorry," I said, lifting it off the floor and handing it back to him with a smile. "I didn't mean to scare you."

Under different circumstances, Jayce would have been a seriously attractive man. He was a chef, clearly driven, young and with a strong jawline. But my heart had been torn to shreds, and being handsome didn't make a person less suspicious.

"What are you doing here?" he asked, taking the lighter from me.

"You seem anxious," I said. "What's wrong?"

"I— I barely know you, why would I—?" He lit his cigarette and inhaled deeply.

"I know that there have been other murders or accidents on board this ship," I said. "So how about you level with me? DId someone die in the freezer?"

Jayce choked on his cigarette and puffed smoke everywhere.

There were times when it was necessary to be blunt and brash and make people uncomfortable.

"Seriously, what's going on? You've been acting strange around me."

"Look, there's nothing to tell," Jayce said loudly, then glanced left and right, and came closer. He drew me aside, a bit of ash dropping off his cigarette and onto the decking below. "If Captain Quinton here's you talking, I'll get fired." His voice was a breathy whisper. "I can't afford to lose this job."

"All right," I said. "Why were you looking out the porthole window earlier?"

"Look," he said. "I don't have much to do with any of this. I came on board after the last 'incident'." He swallowed. "But I heard... Well, I heard rumors."

"What kind of rumors?"

"That Calliope, and that snake tamer, Eve? They were friends with the last man who... The man in the freezer."

"Who was the man in the freezer?"

"I've said too much," Jayce murmured, and sucked on his cigarette. He tapped the ash off, nervously. "Way too much. I was never here." And then he stubbed out his cigarette and rushed for the swinging doors.

For a guy who didn't want anyone to know he was around, he sure hadn't cleaned up after himself. I sighed, picked up his cigarette butt and deposited it into a nearby trash can. I didn't have the contacts to get the DNA tested and certainly not within the next seven days.

Besides, if I called up Special Agent in Charge Grant, he would chew me out for getting involved in something like this.

Maybe it was loneliness driving me, or maybe it was a hunger to find out exactly why or what had happened, but I had to know now.

I tucked my strappy sandals under one arm then took the long leisurely walk back to the guesthouse in the quiet of the night, scanning my surroundings as I went. Even as I tried to remain focused on everything at once, a deep sense of peace settled over me.

It felt good to be out in the open air, living a life away from heartache and pain. Even if it was temporary.

Ten

The following morning, I sat at the table right next to the front window in the Oceanside Guesthouse, my phone in front of me. Last night, I'd downloaded a few books to an app on my phone, and I'd spent time reading them, to distract myself from the corkboard and the furious and sometimes frantic thoughts.

It was tiring to have threads spread and then retract when I realized that there was a dead-end.

Jayce's admission had been fascinating, and I'd decided my time was best spent allowing that information to mull over before I acted on it.

Namely by researching The Emerald Countess like a crazy woman.

Which was the plan this morning.

If there had been an accident on board, then it would've been reported somewhere.

"Everything okay over here?" Sam stopped beside my table, smiling at me. She had on a lovely bright apron that bore the Oceanside Guesthouse's name on the front, and held a coffee pot in one hand.

"It's great," I said. "Actually, I could use a refill." I nudged my cup across the table. "You have a beautiful guesthouse here. You must get a lot of guests."

"We're blessed," Sam said. "It was an uphill struggle at first, but now we're settled in and I couldn't be happier." She poured the coffee for me. "You let me know if you need anything at all. I've got Shawn cooking in the kitchen, so breakfast should be out in a minute. You like croissants, right?"

"Like them? I should be fifty percent croissant at this point." A true fact about me, Delta, rather than April, but I'd allow it.

April's character was meek and mild, sweet and caring. And it was difficult to hold back, sometimes. I understood how my cousin, Charlie, had to feel.

"I hope you get your food truck back soon," Sam said, and sat down at the chair across from mine.

I smiled at her. I didn't mind the interruption. I missed having friends, and she seemed like such a sweet person. "Me too. I can't believe that the first week I'm in a new town, this happens. But it could be worse. I could be the woman who ate the Strawberry Swirl ice cream."

Sam pulled a face. "Funnily enough, this isn't the first time something like this has happened in Carmel Springs."

"Really?"

"Oh yeah," she said. "We had a spate of murders a couple of years back, but it got resolved pretty quickly. With the help of a couple of local heroes."

"Color me intrigued," I said, leaning in.

"Well, they were two women who owned a food truck, funnily enough."

"You're kidding," I said. "What are the odds?"

Sam laughed. "They were great. They stayed here for a while, and we're still in contact. Ruby and Bee. You would've liked them."

"Maybe I can—"

The purr of an engine cut across my words, and both Sam and I looked out the front window. A police cruiser parked out front, and Detective White hopped out and smoothed a hand over his bald crown.

I sighed. "For me."

Sam and I parted ways, and I hurried through to the front of the guesthouse to meet the detective on the porch. I didn't want to disturb the other guests—a family of four on vacation.

"Miss Waters," he said.

"Detective White," I replied. "How can I help you this morning?"

"You're assuming I'm here to see you."

"Presuming, and am I wrong?"

"No," he replied. "Though that's kinda not the point." He murmured something under his breath that sounded suspiciously like "darn leaf peepers." But that couldn't be right, given that it was summer and there were no fall leaves to peep at.

"What's the news?" I asked.

"Your truck," he said. "It's clear. And you are as well. For now."

"For now?"

"We're still working on figuring out what happened."

"The toxicology report didn't tell you what happened?"

"That's really none of your business, Miss Waters." His eyes narrowed. "You can come by the station later to collect your truck."

"Thank you," I said, frowning. "You didn't have to come all the way out here for little old me." So why had he?

"Yeah, well, you're welcome." And then he tipped an invisible hat and walked off toward his cruiser.

I retreated inside to the table at the front and watched him leave. After breakfast, I'd fetch the truck and serve up some ice cream. I had a stipend from the NSIB, but selling the ice cream was part of my cover, and I'd found I enjoyed being on the truck, meeting new people. It would also give my brain a chance to work over the problem.

I had come to learn two things about myself.

I trusted the wrong people—a terrible trait in a spy.

And that forcing myself to focus only made the solution to my problem more illusive.

Sam exited the doors to the Oceanside's kitchen carrying a tray and delivered a hot croissant to my table with a smile. Just the sustenance I'd need to start another interesting day in Carmel Springs.

I SET UP THE FOOD TRUCK OVERLOOKING THE beach, near the boardwalk, and in clear view of the cruise ship. The locals in Carmel Springs were super friendly, stopping by for a much needed ice cream on a hot summer's day. They left the truck with broad smiles and cones topped with scoops of ice cream in vibrant colors.

At noon, a few of the passengers from the cruise ship, notable because of their floral shirts, cameras, and general air of excitement.

Doctor Briggs stopped underneath the blue and pink striped awning, wearing a smile that wrinkled the corners of his eyes. "I've been meaning to stop by for a scoop of ice cream," he said. "What do you recommend?"

Not the Strawberry Swirl. "What are you in the mood for?" I asked.

Doctor Briggs shifted his glasses down his nose. "Everything looks delicious. How about a sugar cone with the Berry Ripple?"

"I can do that for you," I said, and grabbed a sugar cone from the cone dispenser, the plastic gloves I wore crinkling as I worked. "How have you been, Doctor Briggs?"

"Please, call me Doc."

"Doc," I said. "How have you been?"

"Oh, all right. I'm distressed about Angela's passing," he said.

I moved to the Berry Ripple tub, which was half-empty underneath its shimmering glass dome. I scooped some of the ice cream into the cone and added a little extra for good measure before handing it over to Doc.

"Were you good friends with her?" I asked.

"Oh yes," he said. "She was in and out of my office. You see, she had a lot of trouble sleeping, so I was the one who gave her sleeping pills to help her. Night terrors. Poor girl." He shook his head, and he did look genuinely sad. He gestured with his ice cream. "Thanks for this."

"You're welcome." I accepted his payment, and he

strolled off before I got the chance to ask him anything else.

I filed the image of him standing in front of the truck for later dissection, and then my gaze traveled to the cruise ship, with its sleek sides, many windows, and dark wood decks. What was it hiding?

Eleven

Dinner at the Oceanside was one of my favorite parts of the day. Sam and Shawn outdid themselves every night, offering up home-cooked meals with ingredients that were fresh and sourced locally. I sat at my favorite table in the dining room, my phone out, and my hand on the can of Coke Sam had brought me.

The smells from the kitchen, tantalizing, seafood and butter, lemon and garlic, drifted through the quiet dining area. It wasn't time for the guests to be seated yet, but I found sitting here helped set me at ease.

And I had a lot to think about.

I unlocked my phone and opened a new browser tab, then typed in the phrase "The Emerald Countess." The search results held a lot of information on how to book a trip with the cruise line, details about the itinerary, and other mundane tidbits.

I frowned and typed in another phrase. "The Emerald Countess deaths."

The results were sparse, but an article title caught my attention.

The Emerald Countess: Cruise Paradise or Death Trap?

The website that had published it was titled "Conspiracy or Truth".

I tapped on the link, just as the doors to the kitchen swung open and Sam emerged, wiping her hands on her navy blue apron to match the ocean. "There you are, April," she said. "Are you ready for a delicious lobster roll?"

"That would be amazing," I said. "I've always wanted to try one, especially a classic Maine lobster roll."

"It'll be out soon!" And then she was off again, Trouble bounding out from underneath one of the tables and batting at her heels.

I turned my attention back to the article.

There's nothing spookier than a ghost ship. And The Emerald Countess has to be a ghost ship, judging by the sheer number of incidents that have taken place on board.

Of course, nothing has been "proven" but there's evidence and eyewitness accounts to corroborate the stories that have filtered out on social media. So far, there have been three cases of missing persons on board the cruise ship, as well as a death.

Get this, the guy who died, was found in the freezer and was rumored to have been the sous chef. Now, this is one of the only documented tragedies on board The Emerald Countess because the captain of the ship actually made a statement about it, calling it a regrettable tragedy.

Not a murder.

But what about the folks who have gone missing? What happened to them? How can it be possible that a person can go missing while out at sea?

Of the three missing persons cases, or lack thereof, only one has been confirmed by sources on board the cruise ship itself. One of the staff members, who preferred to remain anonymous during their brief chat with me via email, had this to say.

"This is not the kind of holiday you'd expect on board a cruise ship. You come out expecting sun and fun, and all you get is danger. The Emerald Countess seems perfect from the outside, but it's really dangerous. The safety standards on board the ship are low, and it's no surprise that things go

wrong all the time. And that the tickets are so cheap."
Another source, a passenger who preferred that they were not named, had an online video chat with me, and had this to say.

Q: So, you say that things aren't right on board the ship. What do you mean by that?

A: It's something you have to experience for yourself, you know? I've been on board the ship for a few months now, and it's been an interesting time.

Q: Interesting how?

A: It's not safe here, and a lot of the passengers think that the captain is hiding something. He's also not a fan of animals, especially dogs, even though the cruise ship allows them on board.

Q: Have you personally seen anything alarming?

A: Not personally, but the way the staff act is strange. They're really jumpy, and if you ask them anything about what happened on the ship, they refuse to talk.

An image of Hentie talking to this faceless internet guy formed in my mind. I continued reading.

The rest of the article was pretty much the same. The conclusion was that there was definitely something strange happening.

I researched the death of the sous chef on board The Emerald Countess, but apart from a brief statement from the cruise line lamenting the passing of a staff member due to a terrible accident, and a couple of articles about it. No foul play was the official party line, but after what Jayce had said, could that be true?

He'd been suspicious of Eve and Calliope.

An image of the two of them appeared in my mind, Calliope sitting back with a smile on her face and Eve, her hand flat on the table, mid-sentence. A sliver of a thread spread from them toward the image of Jayce and the freezer.

It wasn't a lot to work with, but if the police were determined to let this one go, I was curious. If Angela hadn't died from a bite of ice cream or poisoning or some other nefarious means, then it had to be natural causes.

But after what I'd read and heard on board the cruise ship, that seemed like a huge coincidence.

Sam emerged from the kitchen holding a plate, and I set aside my research for now. That blurry picture on my mental corkboard bugged me. It was almost as if I could see it, but what could the answer be? And who would have wanted to get rid of Angela?

More like, who had hated her the most?

Calliope? Who stood to inherit from her.

Eve? Who had disliked Angela and who might've been in cahoots with Calliope.

Jayce? Who was spying on the pair and had free access to the allegedly poisoned ice cream. Which the police now said wasn't poisoned.

Captain Quinton? Who kept secrets and wanted the cruise ship to leave port.

Hentie? Who said she was friends with the victim, but clearly hadn't been her biggest fan after how Angela had treated Barkington.

Or the mysterious Doctor Briggs who had tried to interfere with the investigation?

"Here you go," Sam said, and set down the lobster roll in front of me.

My mind stopped running away with itself, and I inhaled the delicious scents. Lemon and mayo and lobster —packed onto a toasted bun, with a side of potato chips. "This looks amazing, Sam. Thank you."

"It's a good meal after a long day's work. I hope you enjoy it."

I thanked her again and started on the meal, transported by the flavors, my gaze wandering to the window that looked out on the parking area, and my ice cream truck that awaited.

There had to be a simple explanation for what had happened. And I had an idea about who could help me figure it out.

Twelve

"It's so nice of you to come visit me," Hentie said. "Barkington missed you yesterday." And true to her words, Barkington yipped and struggled to be free of Hentie's grasp. She let him down and he bounded toward me, wagging his tiny tail.

I scooped him up and petted him, and he licked my cheeks. "Hello there," I said, and smiled at the affection. I was more of a cat person, but I loved animals equally and traveling on my ice cream truck didn't offer much of an opportunity for interacting with pets. I soaked up the attention.

"How was breakfast?" I asked.

"Nobody dropped dead," Hentie said. "Which is good news on board this ship."

I nodded and set down Barkington, sweeping my gaze over the interior of Hentie's cabin. It was opulent, decorated in whites and creams, marble with deep mahogany accents—the living room of her suite had glass floor-to-ceiling windows that afforded a view of the ocean and the deck below. Notably, it wasn't a view of the pool deck.

"Yeah, I read an interesting article about that," I said.

Hentie cleared her throat, adjusting the lapels of her neat pants suit—covered in florals today, her hair piled on top of her head. "Ja, about that," she said. "I did what I had to do."

"What are you talking about?"

"Listen, where I come from we call a spade a spade, and we shoot straight," she said. "Meaning, that if you ask me a question, I'm going to tell it to you, like it is." Barkington barked enthusiastically.

Barkington pattered over to join her. He sat at her side like a miniature gargoyle.

"A couple of weeks ago, a guy called me asking to interview me about The Emerald Countess. I agreed, and I gave him one of those internet call interview things."

"Why?"

"Because there's something wrong on board this ship."

"But if there's something wrong," I said, "why are you staying? Why not leave? Go on another cruise ship?"

"Because I'm a sucker for a good mystery. Aren't you? And also, I'm comfortable here, and if I did that, I'd have to phone my hubby and ask him to change my tickets, and it would be a whole thing. Do you want a cup of coffee?" She gestured to her coffee station.

"Sure."

"Don't worry," Hentie said. "I'm not going to poison you."

"That's comforting."

Hentie made a pot of coffee while I paced to the windows that overlooked the deck. Barkington ran around in circles, and eventually went to a group of pee pads Hentie had set up in the corner.

"Here you go." Hentie handed me a cup of coffee. "Listen, I don't know about you, but I'm not the most trusting person around. I'm good at figuring out who to trust, and who's shady. And you, ma'am, are the perfect mix of both."

I wanted to be offended, but she wasn't far off.

"You're so interested in what's going on on the ship, and that's refreshing," Hentie said. "Everyone wants to stick their heads in the sand. Like Jayce."

I took a sip of the coffee. "What about him?"

"He likes to whisper warnings to people," Hentie said. "Did it to me on the first day I boarded the ship. Don't you think that's a little weird? Why's he doing that?" She paused to take a sip from her cup. "Needs more sugar," she muttered, and walked over to the polished wooden table that held the porcelain pot of sugar. "And then there's the doctor." She stirred the sugar through the coffee. "You know, he's the only one on board who liked her."

"Angela?"

"Ja," she said, *tinking* the spoon against the rim of the cup. "He seemed to like Angela quite a bit."

"I got that impression from him as well," I said.

"You see, I think that makes him suspicious because nobody liked Angela. She was... well, she was a complicated woman," Hentie said.

"I thought you two had a mutual agreement, given that you were lifers."

Hentie chewed on the corner of her lip. She set down her cup on the coffee table, then took a seat on the plush cream sofa. Barkington jumped up to join her. "Ja, well, here's the thing." She cleared her throat. "Here's the thing."

"What's the thing?"

"I'm getting to the thing, if you'll give me a minute, I'm just, uh, you know—"

"Stalling?" I asked.

Hentie snorted and Barkington whined and climbed into her lap. "The thing," Hentie said, "is that Angela and I go back further than the ship."

"Care to elaborate?" I sat down across from her, my back to the vast windows, and studied her.

Hentie fiddled with her messy gray hair, pinched one of her eyebrows absently, looked off to one side and back at me. "I suppose it's not a big deal to talk about it, but—" She let out a breath. "Angela and I had a mutual friend."

"Who?"

"My husband's ex-wife."

I did the relationship math on that.

"I know, I know, it sounds strange," Hentie said, "but I'm good friends with Franklin's ex-wife. You see, she's this tiny slip of a thing. Young and pretty, with dark luxurious hair and curves for days. Kind of like you."

I blinked. "Thanks."

"Of course, poppie," she said. "But listen here, this girl, Jocelyn, she was waiting for Franklin to die. She didn't really love him, not like I do, and she got impatient. She fell in love with the pool boy. I was her yoga instructor when it happened."

"This is..."

"Confusing, I know."

"I was going to say unorthodox."

"That's life. Life happens, people do crazy things, and we're all here for the ride," Hentie said, with a wry smile. "Anyways, Jocelyn was the one who introduced me to Franklin, and the rest is history."

"But how is Jocelyn connected to Angela?"

"Distant relations. Jocelyn is Angela's niece on her mother's side," Hentie said. "I met her when I went to Thanksgiving at Jocelyn's house. Franklin was working late, you see, and there wasn't anything else to do."

So, Jocelyn was related to Angela, and that was how Hentie had met the victim.

"Jocelyn was the first person to tell me to stay away from Angela in the first place. They didn't get along, because Angela was a user. Always used to take things from the family." Hentie shrugged. "Anyway, I thought you should know."

"Why?"

"Because I can tell what kind of person you are."

"And what kind of person is that?"

Hentie pinched her eyebrow between her forefinger and thumb, considering. "The type of person who doesn't let go once they get hold of something. It's not a bad trait to have. I mean, you could have just let this go already," she said. "Think about it. You've got your truck back, the police said the cruise ship can leave port, but you're still here, asking questions."

I should have let this go.

But that blurry image on the corkboard wouldn't let me leave. If the police didn't think this was a murder, then how had Angela died?

I rose from my seat. "Thanks for the coffee, Hentie. I'll come by another time."

"Where are you running off to?" she asked.

I shouldn't let her in on that information, but I liked Hentie. I got a good vibe from her. "I've got to see the doctor."

Thirteen

If Angela had been under the weather, or had a pre-existing condition, Doctor Briggs would know about it. Especially since he had "liked" her. But how much had he liked her?

I stopped in front of one of the many sign boards that mapped out the decks on The Emerald Countess, the sounds of children shrieking with joy and the chatter from the cruise ship passengers fuzzing to white noise.

Doctor Briggs' office was on the second deck, one floor below the VIP section, and I headed for the side entrance that led into the magnificent interior of the cruise ship.

I stepped into the sunlit, marble atrium, complete with a glass cupola above, and made for the elevators. A strange squawking noise stopped me in my tracks.

Two people rushed toward me, one of them flapping

their arms. "There you are!" Calliope cried, drifting over in another of those floaty cotton shift dresses.

Eve, the snake charmer from the other night, accompanied her. She lifted a tissue to her nose and let out another squawk. *A sneeze.* Then dabbed under her eyes. She wore an oversized sun hat and shot glances left and right. "Sorry," she said. "I think I'm allergic to something around here. Might be the detergent they're using."

Sick? I took a mental snapshot.

"Good morning," I said, with a bright smile. "How are you today?"

"We've been meaning to catch up with you," Calliope said. "We missed you at breakfast."

"I didn't realize I'd been invited."

"Well, of course you're invited to breakfast." Calliope took me by the arm and walked me away from the elevator as a group of passengers converged on it. "Why wouldn't you be?"

I frowned. "Where's Betty?"

"She's unwell," Eve said, with a shake of her head. "Poor girl started feeling nauseated after dinner last night."

"That's unfortunate. I hope she gets better soon," I said.

"That's what life is like on board a ship like this." Eve squawk-sneezed again, then wiped her nose vigorously.

"Sorry. You work on board this ship, you always run the risk of getting ill."

"Please, Eve, don't sneeze on her," Calliope said. "You're a veritable sack of germs."

"It's allergies." Eve sniffled. "I'm not a sack of germs. I'm in perfect health." She dabbed underneath her red and watering eyes. "Anyway, we wanted to invite you to dinner again."

"I thought you couldn't fraternize with the guests," I said.

"Yes, well, we're undercover." Eve giggled, gesturing to her jeans and shirt, and the oversized floppy hat she's perched on top of her head. "Nobody will recognize me out of my costume."

"And it will be a private dinner," Calliope said, then leaned in and put up a hand. "We're going to have a poker night. Cigars, oysters, and seven-card stud."

"I'm starting to see why Betty's ill," I said. "That sounds like a lethal combo."

"What's wrong with seven-card stud?" Calliope scratched her wrinkled brow.

"I meant the cigars and oysters."

Calliope and Eve cackled and leaned against each other, like I was the opener for the VIP dinner.

"I'm not sure I should attend if you're feeling sick," I said.

"Allergies," Eve repeated.

"It seems like there's something going around on board the ship. If Betty's ill, you've got the—"

"Allergies."

"Sure, the allergies, and I heard that Angela was sick before she passed too," I said.

Calliope's eyes widened.

Eve nodded. "Yeah, I heard about that. But I doubt it's what caused her death."

"You never told me that." Calliope nudged the younger woman. "What do you mean she was ill. Ill with what? How?"

"I don't know the details," Eve said. "I'm not a doctor. I just know she was feeling under the weather. What's the big deal?"

"You've been hacking and sneezing all morning. What if it's a deadly virus?" Calliope put her hand up in front of her mouth.

"Don't be dumb," Eve said. "It's allergies. I told you. Summertime and the cruise ship has been here for a few days. It's all the trees. That's half of the reason I prefer working out at sea. Helps me avoid pollen and—" Eve's eyes widened, and she glanced past my shoulder.

"What is it?" Calliope asked.

"It's *him* again. Ugh."

I turned my head and spotted Jayce, his hair ruffled,

and his chef's whites splodged with stains, ducking out of sight behind a polished wooden door.

"He's still bothering you?" Calliope asked.

"Who is?" Better to play unaware. Eve would give me more detail about Jayce.

"Jayce," Eve sighed. "He's my ex-boyfriend."

"Oh," I said.

"Yeah, he's been glaring at me ever since I broke up with him," Eve sighed, and pulled the rim of her hat down. "I don't understand him. He was the one who pulled away from me, and now that I decided I deserved better, he has a problem with it. I'll never understand men."

"And I'll never understand why you thought it was a good idea to infect us all with your dreaded lurgy," Calliope said, blocking her mouth. "I mean, good heavens, Eve. You know I have a sensitive constitution."

"The only thing that's sensitive is that brain of yours," Eve said.

"What's that supposed to mean?" Calliope snapped, dropping her hand from her mouth. She shook her head and lifted it back up again, taking a step back from her friend.

Eve squawk-sneezed, three in rapid succession, and a group of passing passengers gave her a wide berth.

"See!" Calliope said. "I'm not the only one who thinks you shouldn't be out here."

"You're drawing attention to us," Eve hissed. "If they catch me fraternizing, I'll be in huge trouble."

"That's incredibly ironic, coming from a woman who sounds like a parrot when she sneezes."

The two women bickered, and I drifted away from them. I took a mental image of them, standing together, Calliope a pace away, hand up, shaking her head, and Eve rolling her eyes heavenward, the tissue clutched in her hand.

They were unlikely friends, but then, so were any number of people.

What did they have in common?

I entered the elevator and hit the button that would take me down a level. A couple of passengers joined me, a man and woman, holding hands, their skin sun kissed, both of them wearing the smiles of newlyweds. My heart turned and squeezed, and I looked away.

I'd never thought I would fall in love, not even as a girl. When the other girls my age had been dreaming of the perfect husband, or planning their careers as ballerinas or paleontologists, I'd been completely focused on becoming like my great-aunt.

A spy. A spy so brilliant, nobody else would compare.

The memory of my first meeting with Georgina Mission was vividly implanted in my mind. The scent of her perfume, the way she'd sized me up and found me intriguing, and then how she'd left in the dead of the night. The only sign she'd ever been at our house was the book she'd left on my bedside table.

A copy of Sherlock Holmes with a note inside.

You are special, no matter what they say.

And I had never forgotten it.

The elevator doors opened, and I left the couple to their honeymoon, my gaze focused on the distant door to Doctor Brigg's office at the end of the hall.

Fourteen

Doctor Briggs' office door had a silver plaque bearing his name. I lifted my hand to knock, but paused at the muffled sound of talking inside.

"—that's a good idea?" Briggs' smooth tone carried through the wood.

I glanced back up the hall to check no one was on their way down and found the coast was clear.

"Are you questioning me, Nick?" The voice was stiff and familiar. Captain Quinton. "You know I always make choices that are in the best interests of our passengers."

"But what about the crew, sir? And the police?"

"That's been dealt with appropriately," Quinton said. "You don't need to worry about that."

"I'm not worried, I just—"

"If you're not worried, then why did you call me to your office to discuss our departure date?"

"It seems like such a rash decision. Leaving in 48 hours? I don't know, I—"

"While you sit here equivocating, I make decisions that are far above your paygrade. So, you'll forgive me if I don't spend an extra minute on this ridiculous conversation."

That was my cue.

I moved to the door beside Doctor Briggs' office, opened it, and slipped inside. I'd wound up in a closet stacked with cleaning supplies.

A second later, the door to the doctor's office slammed, and Captain Quinton emerged, fixing his white captain's hat onto his well-coiffed hair. He shot a glance to the left and right, eyes narrowed and searching, and then walked off.

I waited two breaths then exited my hiding spot and made for the office.

A knock later, I entered Doctor Brigg's space. He sat behind a vast walnut desk, his head in his hands, staring down at a neat stack of papers atop it. The room was clinical, with white tiles, and matching walls, and an open doorway to the left looked in on an examination room with a bed covered in blue sheets.

If Captain Quinton wanted the ship to set sail in the next two days, my time was limited. I had to make this happen, fast, and with the police clearly not taking this seriously, I was the only one left who could figure it out before the ship sailed off into the sunset.

"Doc?"

His head snapped up. "Oh, uh— April, right. Hi. What are you doing here?"

"Are you all right?" I asked. "You look stressed."

"You could say that," he said. "Did you knock?"

"Yes, I did, sorry. I wanted to check on you."

"Check on me?"

"Yeah," I said. "You were upset the other day."

"Oh right, when I came to grab some ice cream?" He scratched a hand across his forehead and ran it through his graying hair. He couldn't be much younger than Angela had been at the time of her passing, and he'd liked her. "Sorry, April, I'm out of it at the moment. I don't mean to be rude. Usually, I like it when people come to visit me. You know, I only ever see people when they're sick."

"Sure. I should have brought you some ice cream, but I figured it would melt by the time I got here. I'm sorry for your loss."

"My loss," he said.

"Yes, Angela. Sorry if it's presumptuous, but I figured that you two were close, or you liked her because you were upset about her passing. Everyone else seems unaffected. Or kind of happy, to be honest."

"She did have a reputation, didn't she?" Doc smiled. "For, you know, being difficult. But she wasn't a bad person. As for liking her, well, it wasn't like that. She was a patient." He rose from his seat. "Would you like something to drink? Some coffee? Tea?"

I considered it. If anyone could poison me, it would be the doctor. "I'm good, thank you. Don't get up on my account."

"It helps to keep busy," he murmured, and moved to the coffee pot behind his desk. He made the coffee with his back to me.

"You said Angela was your patient."

"Oh yes, well, most people are, given that I'm the only one they can talk to when they're sick. But Angela, yes, she was feeling a little sick before... You know."

"Did she have the flu?" I asked. "I saw one of the other guests had it. Could be contagious."

"Nothing like that, no. She had a little bit of trouble sleeping because she had—" He paused and gestured to his throat. "A post-nasal drip. Just some allergies. Nothing serious. I visited her in her room to prescribe some medication. Although, she did have nausea in the days before her passing."

"Nausea," I said.

"Yes," he replied. "I assume it was because of the post-nasal drip. Some abdominal pain. I gave her meds for all of it and— Goodness, why are you interested?"

"Just because I saw some of the other passengers feeling ill and I was concerned." I laughed, putting up my hands. "You got me. I'm one of those types. Germophobes."

The suspicion on Doc's face faded. "Right, of course. That's understandable. You know, cruise ships like this are a hotbed for germs."

I pulled a face. "Don't tell me that," I said. "I'll have to shower in sanitizer when I get back to the guesthouse."

Doc laughed, and his facial features softened, the lines smoothed a little as he poured himself a cup of coffee. "Is that all you came for today? Just to check that I was okay?"

"Yeah," I said. "I was worried. I don't know, I've been hearing a lot of strange things about this ship, and it doesn't sit right with me that the police aren't *really* investigating Angela's death. They seem relaxed about the whole thing."

Doc nearly choked on his sip of coffee and put his mug down. "I happen to agree with you. It's happening so fast. And this isn't the first time we've had an accident of this nature, especially one like... Like this."

"What do you mean?"

"A while ago, one of the crew members locked themselves in the freezer and, well, it's awful, but he died."

"That *is* awful."

Doc nodded. "Yeah, he had taken too many sleeping pills, gone down for a late night snack, and wound up locking himself in the freezer. It was quite the mystery. There were rumors that the ship would be grounded, but of course, Captain Quinton wouldn't allow that." His jaw clenched then released. "Anyway. In the end, it turned out to be an accident. I blamed myself for it for a long time. I prescribed those sleeping pills you know, and for a moment, I thought something similar had happened to poor Angela, but no... Apparently not. The police haven't even talked to me about it."

"They barely questioned me," I said. "And she took a bite of my ice cream before she died."

"Maybe it was natural causes after all." But Doc's wrinkled brow said he wasn't sure.

"You come by the truck later. I have a Berry Ripple sugar cone with your name on it."

"Thanks, April," he said. "I might just take you up on that offer."

I said goodbye then slipped out into the hall and started walking, removing my phone from my pocket. I shot a text off to Hentie.

Which room did Angela stay in?

Fifteen

I wasn't big on trusting people, but Hentie was my only source of information. And she'd come through with the room number for Angela.

I moved swiftly through the gorgeous hallways, past the food court, the stores, and toward the elevator. I took it up to the VIP deck then stepped out, checking the coast was clear. Betty and Calliope would likely be in their favorite gossip spot overlooking the pool deck, so I took a swift right.

Angela had stayed in a luxury suite that overlooked that deck—could that be the reason for her obsession with the pool towels on the deck chairs? I stopped in front of her door, my mind fuzzing over that fact.

There was something there... What was it?

I checked the coast was clear. The camera that haunted

the corner of the hall was pointed in a different direction. It scanned left and right, and I timed it. One minute to break in. There were passengers lounging on the pool deck below, and a couple passed by, chatting to each other. I leaned on the railing.

Once they were gone, I approached the door to Angela's room—1207—and tried the handle. It was locked, of course, but it was always better to check, in my experience.

I slipped my hand into the front pocket of my jeans and removed two of the most important pieces of my lockpicking set—a rake and a tensioner.

I carried them with me at all times, because there were two things a girl should always have. The potential to get into places she didn't belong and pepper spray.

After that, I removed a pair of latex gloves from my back pocket and snapped them on.

I waited for the camera to turn away, then moved to the door. I dropped to my knees in front of it and picked the lock. It took me ten seconds to get the lock open— terrible security combined with my affection for getting into hard-to-reach places—and I slipped inside and shut the door behind me.

"All right," I breathed. "Let's see what we've got." I stowed my tools in my pocket again then moved through the suite.

Much like Hentie's, it had a gorgeous view of the deck below, through floor-to-ceiling windows. Unlike hers, it was a mess. Angela hadn't cleaned up after herself, and it seemed housekeeping hadn't come in since her passing, possibly because the cops had told them not to?

But if that was the case, why weren't they stopping the ship from departing?

I strode through the interior of the luxury cabin, ignoring the cream carpeting, the crystal vases full of dying flowers, and entered Angela's bedroom. The bed was unmade, the sheets rumpled, and there was a bucket on the floor next to the bed.

Nausea.

I peered inside and recoiled.

And vomiting.

Nausea, vomiting, unable to sleep, post nasal drip? Allergies? Sea sickness?

But nobody had ever died of sea sickness.

I entered the bathroom and opened the cupboards underneath the marble sink. There were plenty of meds inside, and I removed my phone and snapped pictures of them. I'd have to research them later once I was out.

The bathroom was empty of clues, apart from the meds, so I re-entered the bedroom and searched around. Angela's phone was missing, but a laptop sat on the walnut desk overlooking the ocean and deck below—more windows, though the curtains were drawn in here. I clicked on the bedside lamp.

"What do we have here?" I opened the laptop, tapped a few keys, and the screen came to life.

Angela had a password.

And for every problem there was a solution. I slipped my phone from my jeans, opened it, and scrolled through to the app on my phone I'd created specifically for moments like this. I opened the app, pointed my camera at the screen and tapped a few buttons.

Five seconds later, the app pinged with the answer.

Ihatechihuahuas

"Really, Angela?" I typed in the password.

And I was in, the laptop's contents bare before me.

Email was first, but Angela's recent threads were relatively boring. A few discussions between friends, but mostly spam, and nothing alarming. But there was a document on Angela's desktop which she'd labeled as "THE PLAN."

I tapped on the laptop mousepad to open it.

THE PLAN

1. *Go on the cruise. Leave before they can figure out what happened.*

2. *Message Jocelyn once I am out to sea and claim that I am sick.*

3. *Fake death.*

My eyes widened.

I read the note again.

Fake death?

No. Surely not.

But that would've been the perfect way to fake a death. One bite of an ice cream and keel over? And it would explain why the cops weren't investigating.

No. No, it wouldn't.

Because if Angela had faked her death, why would the cops play along? They wouldn't. They would sue her for wasting police time and resources. Unless she'd paid off the coroner and the cops and everyone in the town, but I doubted that she had enough money for that.

Or did she?

I snapped an image of the note using my phone, then exited it, and shut the laptop.

Jocelyn was involved?

She was Hentie's connection to Angela, which brought the whole thing back to my only friend on board this cruise ship. Everything seemed interconnected, but loose and strange at the same time.

There had to be a reason for that.

I hurried from the room and toward the door, then checked my watch. I had been inside for approximately five minutes. Which meant I needed to wait another thirty seconds for the camera to rotate.

I counted it down then exited and shut the door behind me. The camera faced in the other direction exactly as I'd calculated. I strode down the deck, snapping off my gloves, my suspicions growing with each step.

I disposed of the gloves in a metal trash receptacle near the stairs, keeping my pace up, heading toward Hentie's room.

Had Angela faked her death?

She had definitely been ill.

If she'd faked her death, she'd had a reason for it. Which meant she was on the run from someone who would want her dead. Could it be Jocelyn? If that was the case, then was Hentie the one who had killed her?

Either she'd faked the whole thing, which was unlikely —it would take a lot of organization to pull that off—or she'd died at the hands of someone who had known her secret. But what was the secret? What was Angela hiding from?

The thoughts developed in my mind, and I stalled to a halt, leaning a hand on the railing for a second to think it over.

Angela had died or faked her death. Hentie and Jocelyn.

Sickness. But how?

And then there was that darn picture in my brain. It was still slightly out of focus, so that I couldn't figure out how it connected to the image of Angela, dead on the deck.

There was an answer to this.

I had to find it.

Sixteen

I WAS LUCKY THAT THE CAPTAIN HAD BEEN KIND enough to afford me access to The Emerald Countess as a thank you for the ice cream catering at the party—apart from my actual pay. It meant I had full access to the ship, and even the VIP deck.

I strolled along, trying to look casual, even though my thoughts bordered on obsessive about Angela and what I'd discovered.

Hentie had mentioned their mutual friend, but she hadn't mentioned anything about Angela wronging Jocelyn.

Angela's "PLAN" wasn't flawless either. But reading it had given me more questions than answers.

I stopped in front of Hentie's cabin door and lifted a hand to knock.

"Is this why you called me to your cabin?" Doc's voice came from inside, shaking a little. "To accuse me of things that you know nothing about?"

"I know plenty about this," Hentie said. "I know what type of woman Angela was. I know that she was having an affair, and I know that it was with you. So, ja, how about you stop acting like you don't understand why—"

"Stop it. You don't know anything about her. About us."

"So you admit it," Hentie said, triumph in her tone. Barkington barked in the background. "You were in love with her. You were having an affair."

"Even if we did enjoy each other's company, what does that matter? What business is it of yours?"

"It's my business because somebody killed her," Hentie said. "And I'm gonna find out who."

I arched an eyebrow. Looked like I wasn't the only sleuth hanging around. But did Hentie want to solve the murder because she was interested? Because she believed in justice? Or did she have an ulterior motive?

"You're unbelievable," Doc said. "I'm leaving."

"Doctor Briggs, wait." Hentie's voice trembled. "I'm not trying to offend you, but I want to know what happened. A woman is dead, and it isn't the first time something like this has happened on board the ship. I'm a lifer. I'm going to be on board for a long time to come, so you can understand why I would be concerned about—"

"I can understand it," Doc said. "It doesn't mean I agree with your line of questioning or your approach. Nor does it mean I have to respond to your questions. How about you stay out of this? Let the police handle it."

"The police aren't going to do anything about it, and you know that," Hentie said. "Captain Quinton's done something that's made them back off."

"Whatever's going on, it's not my business. Not any more," Doc said.

Before the conversation could get out of hand, I knocked on the door.

Hentie cleared her throat and Barkington launched into a flurry of obsessive barks. The door opened, and Doc gave me a tight smile before squeezing past me and walking off down the deck. I met Hentie's gaze.

"April," she said. "Nice to see you—"

"You think Doc was having an affair with Angela?" Barkington rushed to lick my ankles, and I bent and petted him.

Hentie hesitated. "An affair? Well, Angela's husband was dead, so—"

"And you would know, wouldn't you?" I asked, lifting Barkington into my arms. I entered Hentie's cabin and tapped the door shut with my foot.

"What do you mean?"

"You seem very invested in what happened to Angela, for someone who wasn't exactly her closest friend."

"Ja, but that doesn't mean anything. Inquiring minds like to know. And I told you, I'm invested in what happens on board the ship because I spend most of my time—"

"Tell me the truth, Hentie," I said. "What do you know about Jocelyn and Angela's relationship?"

"They were friends." But Hentie wet her lips. "Goodness, I need some lipstick. I'm getting chapped."

"They were friends," I repeated, while Barkington licked my fingers and tried to encourage me to stroke him.

Hentie hesitated and walked toward the coffee station. "Would you like some—?"

"Tell me what happened between them," I said. "Angela did something to Jocelyn didn't she?"

Hentie's hand trembled so that the coffee pot shook in her hand and she had to put it down.

"Tell me."

"It's difficult for me to discuss, *jong*. You don't understand what it's been like being on board a ship with her when she did—" Hentie cut off and bowed her head. She let out a breath and stroked her hands over the jacket of her neat pants suit then faced me. "Ja, I'm invested. I'm interested in what happened, and it's not just because of Angela being a lifer and this ship being full of mysteries that nobody wants to solve. It's not just because the ship is leaving in a couple of days."

"Then why?"

"Because Jocelyn was wronged by Angela," Hentie said, swallowing audibly. "When I first met Angela, she and Jocelyn were pretty close because they moved in the same circles. Angela was married to a rich man, and given that Jocelyn had been married to my Franklin, they'd become friends. It was an unlikely friendship by anybody's standards."

"What happened?" Barkington wriggled in my arms, and I put him down. He pattered off toward the kitchenette and lapped up water from a tiny silver bowl, emblazoned with his name. "Barkington the Blaf."

"She was good friends with Angela until, well, Angela stole from her," Hentie said.

"You're kidding."

"I'm really not. Angela stole from Jocelyn. She got her to invest in this makeup scheme thing, and Jocelyn was so excited about it. She thought it was going to be her next big thing, especially since she'd just gotten divorced from my Franklin." Hentie waved a hand. "Oh don't worry, he pays her alimony, but she wanted a business of her own. Still does."

"And Angela lied to her about it?"

"Angela took all of her money and promised that she'd

give Jocelyn the products to sell to others. But she never did. It turns out, that makeup company doesn't even exist, and it was a fake site."

"Is that why you're on board?"

"No." Hentie said. "I came on board because I enjoy cruising, and Franklin's so busy we hardly ever see each other, which suits me fine, of course. But when I saw her on board, it made me furious."

Furious enough to kill? I didn't say it out loud, but it lingered in the air.

Hentie shook her head. "I thought, you know what? How dare she? How dare she come on board this cruise ship with my friend's money? The trouble is, or was, that Jocelyn didn't believe that she stole her money."

"She didn't?"

"No," Hentie said. "She kept telling Jocelyn that there were shipping delays with the product, and this was normal, and so on, but I knew the truth. It was a lie, and she took Jocelyn's money."

"Did you tell her?"

"I tried a video chat on my laptop," Hentie said, "but she was convinced it was a big misunderstanding."

"And you don't think so."

"I know it's not. Angela's husband had too many debts when he died. She wanted to escape," Hentie said. "And now, she's— Well, I can't help wondering if this is real? What if Angela found another way out of paying up?"

"You think she faked it?"

Hentie threw up her hands. "I want to know why this has happened. For me. And for Jocelyn." She took a few steps toward me and stopped, her eyes glittering like hard green jewels. "I don't have a lot of friends, so when I make them, I defend them with everything I have. I'm going to figure out what happened. I want my friend to get her money back."

Seventeen

I sat up in bed well past midnight at the Oceanside, the puffy comforter covering my legs, my back supported by comfy pillows. I liked the guesthouse, but it reminded me of what it had been like at the Gossip Inn, in Texas.

My stomach clenched at the thought.

I missed my family, and I missed Mickey. And I couldn't go back. I couldn't ever see them again.

Hentie's insistence on doing what was right for her friend made a lot of sense to me. I could sympathize, even if I wished I could turn off that part of myself. But that would make me a sociopath.

I snorted at my silliness and turned my attention back to my rose gold laptop. It was a new addition to my cover for April—cutesy and sweet, and I adored it. I liked girly things, because I'd spent so much time around guys that pinks and puppies and all things sweet made me happy.

A scratching came at my bedroom door, and I got up to answer it.

Trouble, the guesthouse's ginger cat, gamboled into the room and came to an abrupt stop on the rug between the armchairs. He arched his back and did a little sideways walk.

"Joining me for some late night zoomies?"

He leaped onto my coffee table, chased his tail, then sped off, kicking up the magazines that Sam had placed there as decoration.

I laughed and shut my door then returned to my bed. I shifted the curtain back from the window that was next to it, giving myself a view of the side of the inn, the soft sand, the moonlight.

Beautiful. And then I set to work.

This afternoon, the minute I'd gotten back from the cruise ship, I had crafted an email to the office of the local medical examiner and the police department, requesting the autopsy report for Angela. I'd requested it using a fake email and Calliope's name.

It was a law that next of kin could request the report as long as the death was natural causes.

I opened my email and found the reply waiting.

Dear Mrs. Benson,

Thank you for your inquiry. Unfortunately, we're unable to grant you access to the report at this time as this is an ongoing investigation. I'll refer you to Detective White, who will be happy to answer any questions you have at this time.

Sincerely,

Doctor Taylor

Darn, so they weren't going to give me the report. And that meant that this wasn't natural causes—one possibility ruled out.

But there was the distinct chance that this wasn't a murder at all, and that Angela had managed to fake her death. Would that explain why Captain Quinton had convinced the detective to let the ship go? Or was there more to it than that?

Was it possible that I could get into the morgue and see the body for myself? It was a pretty grim thought, but I needed proof that Angela was dead.

I opened my phone and scrolled until I found the image of the meds I'd found in Angela's bathroom cabinet.

They were as Doc had described.

Sleeping pills. Anti-nausea pills.

So, she definitely had been sick at the time, even if her plan had stated that she'd fake sickness and her death.

That was a *huge* coincidence, if that was the case.

"But what could have caused her death?" I muttered.

Trouble leaped onto the bed and darted over my laptop, his paws typing a nonsensical phrase into my search bar.

I laughed and tried to catch him, but he was off again in a heartbeat.

If she was dead, *actually* dead, then something had killed her. If it was an illness, they wouldn't have been investigating it. If it was poison, they wouldn't have returned my truck.

There were two options.

She had been murdered and they were still trying to figure out the murder weapon and murderer.

She had faked it.

I had to find a way to either prove or disprove either of these theories.

Angela's symptoms could have been a result of sea sickness, of allergies, or any number of things that might have led to her death. There wasn't enough information to go on. Maybe if I broke into Doc's office and got my hands on his files?

Or maybe if I cased out Detective White's house, I'd overhear or see something that might lead to another clue?

I had plenty of clues, but the problem was that all of

those clues pointed in different directions, and my cork-board wasn't helping.

The ice cream hadn't been poisoned. She had been sick for a while. The police were still investigating.

Captain Quinton wanted the ship to leave in a day, now. My time was fast running out to find the truth about all of this. I pushed off the bed and started toward my closet.

I didn't have the body or the report, but I had plenty of suspects who'd been around at the time. If I could rule them out, I'd be able to get to the bottom of this.

Hurriedly, I dressed in all black while Trouble zoomed around in the bedroom.

If she'd been murdered, then I had my suspects, including Hentie. No matter what she said, she wasn't cleared of suspicion, even if she was an interesting person. And surprisingly forthright about what was on her mind.

But without a real cause of death, how was I ever going to figure out who was the murderer? There was no trail of evidence.

Only the trail of destruction Angela had left in her wake.

And that's exactly where I have to start.

I slipped out of my room, waiting with the door open for Trouble to leave, and then headed for the front of the inn. Time was running out. If I planned on finding who'd done this, I had to do it now.

The night was eerily quiet, broken only by the distant rush of waves crashing against the sand.

I started toward my food truck, but a prickle spread across the back of my neck. A feeling I trusted after years in my line of work.

I continued walking, acting as if I hadn't noticed anything and drew my keys out of my pocket. I hummed under my breath, swinging the keys on their keyring easily, my eyes dancing left and right until I found it.

Or rather *him*.

A man standing just near the back of the food truck, watching me. He wore a black hoodie and peeked around the side of the truck.

I kept on humming and unlocked the truck, walking around the front to the driver's side door. I opened it and feigned fiddling with something on the car seat. Footsteps crunched behind me and stopped.

Now.

I spun around and released a rapid series of punches to the man's solar plexus.

He gasped for air and doubled over, but I grabbed him by the arm and twisted it behind his back, pinning it upward so that he cried out.

"S-Stop," he wheezed. "P-Please."

"Who are you?" I hissed.

Eighteen

"Who are you?" I repeated.

The man squeaked and froze. He couldn't move without breaking his arm, and he stood there, panting. "It's just me," he said. "Jayce."

"Any reason you were walking up behind me in the dark, wearing a hoodie, Jayce?" I asked.

Why would he want to hurt me, unless he'd realized I was investigating the case? But he was the one who'd come to me and told me about the corpse in the freezer and the previous accident on board the ship.

Jayce let out great huffs of air. "I wasn't going to hurt you."

"No," I said. "You don't have the capability to hurt me. There's a difference."

"Let me go, please."

"Why should I? You came here in the middle of the night. If you wanted to see me, you could have knocked on the front door of the inn."

"And wake everyone up?"

"That's what you're worried about? Not the potential lawsuit from trying to attack me in the middle of the night?" I jerked on his arm, and he let out a shout.

"Please! I wasn't going to hurt you. I wanted to talk."

"Talk."

"I—"

I shoved him forward so that he stumbled. "Tell me what you want."

Jayce turned toward me, massaging his shoulder. He grimaced as he pulled his hood down. "I wanted to talk to you," he said. "It's important."

"So you approached me from behind without saying a word because you wanted to talk to me." Out of habit, I kept weapons stashed in the truck and on my person. I had a gun underneath the driver's seat, safely stowed in its holster on an attached rack. One of many.

"It's not like that," Jayce said. "Look. I didn't want to cause any trouble. I didn't want to be seen."

"Seen by who? Me, I assume."

"No," he said. "By..." He took two tentative steps forward. "By *them*."

"I'm going to need more than that." I breathed easily, my gaze fixed on him, taking in his movements, the way he shifted his weight, scanning him for threats or weapons. He'd let go of his shoulder, but he worked it occasionally.

"They're all preoccupied at a party at the moment. Drinking and laughing in the VIP dining room."

"Yeah, sure, but who are you hiding from?"

"The captain," he hissed. "He's up to something. I know that he's involved in what happened to Angela."

I lifted my palms. "What do you mean?"

"It can't be a coincidence," Jayce said, glancing around and taking another tentative step toward me. "I mean, think about it. How come two people have died on board the ship recently? Why is the ship leaving in one day when there was a woman who just died on board? You seemed interested in this stuff when I saw you the other day. You wanted to know."

"Yes," I said. "I want to know."

"Then I can tell you that... that there is something *wrong* with Captain Quinton. I don't like or trust him, and he runs the ship like he's a captain in the military rather than it being a normal luxury cruise ship. He wants everyone to bow down to him."

"You've mentioned this before," I said, leaning against the side of the truck, making sure that my gun was well within reach. "But you're not really saying anything new.

You think he likes attention and there's something wrong with him, but what does that mean, Jayce? What's wrong with him?"

He gnawed on his bottom lip. "I think he's behind it. I don't know why. Maybe he likes to kill people. Maybe that's it."

That was a leap in reasoning for sure. And it was a bit outlandish, even for a woman like me. The captain being some sort of sea-roaming serial killer was unlikely. There would be too many people involved in that type of cover-up.

The simplest answer was often the true one.

So how could Angela have possibly faked her death? She'd have needed to involve countless people, and have a lot of money, and the truth was, if she'd stolen from Jocelyn, she probably didn't have enough money or friends.

Hearsay.

Jayce was silent, staring at me, waiting for me to respond to his accusation.

"You think that Captain Quinton killed Angela?" I asked.

"Yes," he said. "It sounds crazy, but that's exactly what I think. He didn't like that she stole the limelight, so he decided to get rid of her." Jayce stuffed his hands into the pockets of his hoodie. "Remember that night at the party?

Angela was out of hand, loud and angry, and Captain Quinton hated it. I saw the look on his face."

I had a mental image of the look Quinton had worn when he saw how the other passengers reacted to me saving Barkington, but that didn't prove anything. The man could want attention, that didn't make him a raging murderer.

And I had to consider the source, because Jayce was a suspect too. His oddball behavior had seated him firmly in that territory, and the fact that he was so invested. Not everyone on board this ship could be a sleuth. So why was he interfering?

"I'm telling you, he's a killer," Jayce continued. "He didn't like the last sous chef so he got rid of him and staged it to look like a murder."

"Do you have any proof?" I asked.

It would be a good tactic for a murderer to point the finger at someone else.

"No," Jayce said. "But I think he had help."

"What kind of help?" I asked.

"From his new girlfriend." Jayce's lips drew into a thin slash. "Eve."

"The snake tamer?"

"Yeah, her. She's his new girlfriend. Not many people know about it, but she's been fraternizing with the captain for weeks now."

"But you dated her, didn't you?"

Jayce froze. "Who told you that?"

"She did," I said.

"You— You're friends with her?" He backed up several steps.

"Not friends with her, no. But she mentioned it. That you and her were dating. How could she have helped Captain Quinton kill anyone if you dated her before she dated him, and the first death predated your arrival on board The Emerald Countess."

Jayce's mouth opened and closed. "I—Yeah, but she's helping him now."

"So he was murdering people before she started dating him?"

More blank looks. He took another few steps back. "Look, just, uh, forget I said anything. I've got to go." And then he turned and ran off, pulling his hood up as he went, his sneakers scraping against the sidewalk.

Jayce was out to get Eve. That or he truly believed she was behind it. Either Eve was lying about them having dated, or Jayce was lying about everything. And where did the captain and Hentie fit into this? And Calliope?

If this was a murder, then she'd benefited from Angela's passing the most. But if Angela had needed money, then surely her husband hadn't left her much of it in the first place.

Secrets. So many secrets.

It seemed like everyone on board The Emerald Countess had something to hide.

Nineteen

I boarded the cruise ship quietly, the keys to my truck in one pocket, the other keeping another pair of latex gloves and my lockpicking tools. If Gamma Mission had taught me anything, it was the importance of being prepared—and of the element of surprise.

The cruise ship was alive with noise and activity, though it was late at night. The sound of music, of people having fun drew me along the deck.

The party was in full swing in the VIP dining room, and I stopped to check inside on my way toward Calliope's rooms. Since I'd had to check out Angela's, I'd made a point of finding out where everyone stayed from Hentie.

Calliope and Betty sat at their usual table, but they weren't alone tonight. Captain Quinton was with them, clutching a glass of champagne and laughing at something Calliope had said. The dining room was full of laughter and raucous guests—a few had started dancing between the tables.

They were totally distracted.

I scanned the space for the staff. Eve was nowhere to be seen, but that was to be expected since she wasn't allowed to fraternize with the guests. Funny how Captain Quinton was allowed to, but the other crew members weren't.

I left them to their party and headed out of the door, moving fast without breaking into a run.

Calliope's room was around the corner from Hentie's, the entrance was inside the ship rather than easy access to the deck. The camera at the end of the hall was fixed in position, though, so I strode past it. Once I was in its blind spot, I grabbed a chair from a nearby set of armchairs for guests to lounge in, and scooted it beneath the camera.

Hurry.

I climbed onto the chair, lifted my phone, and hacked the camera's system—wi-fi—disabling it. When security came to check on the camera, they'd find it was undamaged and assume that this was a technical glitch.

The "glitch" gave me ten minutes to get into Calliope's room and find evidence that either proved or disproved her involvement in the murder.

I pushed the chair back into place then darted down the hall, my hands in my pockets, already grasping for my lockpicking set.

The lock was similar to Angela's—easy to get past—and I entered Calliope's luxury suite a minute later.

Nine minutes left.

The room was as gorgeous as Angela's, but with accents of rich red and gold. I didn't have time for the view or to admire the decor. I moved through the space with purpose.

There had to be something. Anything in this room that would help me.

Calliope didn't have a laptop. And her phone was likely in her purse.

The rooms were incredibly neat too. If I left anything out of place, Calliope would notice.

Eight minutes.

I checked under the bed, in the bathroom cabinets, snapping pictures of the pills, searching. Searching. But for what?

Seven minutes.

The luxury living room was empty of interesting items. Even the coffee table was bare, apart from the cruise ship's entertainment itinerary. I picked it up and arched an eyebrow.

Calliope has specifically circled Eve's portion of the

evening's entertainment. And the Captain's party—VIPs only. I snapped a picture of that.

Five minutes.

I ran into the bedroom again, opened the closet and found plenty of coats and dresses, even pairs of white evening gloves. But nothing of note, except—

"What's this?" I switched on the light in the walk-in closet.

One of the shelves near the back was empty of shoes. A book rested on it, shoved back almost like it was supposed to be hidden.

Four minutes.

I opened it and grinned.

Calliope's journal.

Hurriedly, I snapped pictures of the pages, as many of them as I could, and then I rifled through them myself. Committing them to memory. My brain was capable of it, taking note of where the words were situated.

The pictures on my phone were for evidence. The pictures in my mind for later perusal.

I shut the journal and pressed it into the corner where I'd found it, my latex gloves crinkling.

Two minutes.

I turned off the lights as I moved through the suite then opened the door, checked the coast was clear, and slipped out into the hall.

One minute.

I stripped my gloves off and walked away, rounding the corner out of sight of the camera, just as it came back online, a smile parting my lips.

§

BACK AT THE OCEANSIDE, I PACED BACK AND forth in my room in the dead of the night. Trouble had followed me back into my bedroom and lay across the end of the bed, purring and stretching out his little calico paws to massage the comforter.

"You know," I said, stopping to look at him. "Male calico cats are super rare. The chances you exist are about 1 in 3,000. That makes you special."

He yawned at me, unconcerned by the factoid.

And I didn't blame him, but I needed a second to process the information I had gleaned from Calliope's journal. And what the implications of the information might be.

I sat down next to Trouble and stroked his head. He squeezed his eyes shut and stretched out, then pulled his paws to his face. Adorable.

"Okay," I said. "Here goes nothing." I shut my eyes and explored my memories.

Instead of turning to the corkboard with its pictures, I

moved toward the journal that lay on the shelf in peaceful darkness.

I opened it and paged through it. There were only a few pages at the front that were blurred because of my rush to get in and out of the suite without being seen.

"What do we have here," I murmured, flicking the pages in my mind, my finger tapping on the bed beside me in real time.

> What an awful day. I can't tell you how sick I am of Angela's behavior. She's such a spoiled brat and I can't believe anyone would want to be friends with her. Betty and I both agreed that she's obviously just very good at manipulating people. Why else would Hentie be friends with her? Or Doctor Briggs, for heaven's sake? I'll never understand it.

I turned another page.

> I've been talking to both Eve and Betty about her behavior and we've decided that something has to be done about it. Just the other day, Angela made a point of targeting

Eve in front of the Captain. She told that arrogant man that she thought snakes were boring and there were better sources of entertainment for the guests. Can you believe that? Of course you can't. Because you're a journal. Ha.

More Angela hate from Eve and Betty. Motive for Eve? Another page turned.

We've come up with a plan to put her in her place. I'm not going to write it down here, but Eve and I have come up with a solution to our little problem. I can't wait to see the look on Angela's face. It will serve her right for the way she treated my brother. It will serve her right for the harm she's done.

What was that about? Serve her right?

Rumors are spreading about Angela. Hentie seems to have pulled back from being her friend, but I wonder if we can trust her enough to tell her our plan. Eve says we shouldn't involve more people than necessary, even if it's a prank, but I think the more the merrier. It's just a joke.

What was a joke? What plan had these women hatched to get back at Angela?

Twenty

I'D STRUGGLED TO SLEEP AFTER READING Calliope's journal.

I grabbed a bite to eat at the Oceanside—two strong cups of coffee and eggs on toast with bacon and fried green tomatoes on the side—and then headed out. The ice cream truck, with its ever-dripping ice cream cone on top, and the vinyl print on the side that had dripping lettering—I Scream for Ice Cream—brought a smile to my lips.

I'd never thought I'd enjoy serving ice cream on a food truck, but it was fun. The truth was, I'd been avoiding it all week because of the memories I had of my last food truck and my late ex, Mickey.

I darted up the ramp toward the entrance to the cruise ship, nodding to security as I passed, and made straight for the top floor and the VIP decks. A couple of minutes later, I knocked on Hentie's suite door.

Silence.

Maybe she'd taken Barkington to breakfast?

I knocked again, in case they were sleeping in, then turned toward the pool deck, lifting my hand to my brow to shield my eyes from the morning sun. There were a few cruise passengers wandering around or sunning themselves on the deck, and a group of kids splashed each other in the pool, screeching and laughing.

A memory threatened.

I was twelve again, watching the girls I went to school with play in the public pool. My mother's hand rested on my shoulder, and she squeezed tight. *"You don't really think they want to play with you, do you? Why would they, Delta? You're weird. Just like your father."*

"April!" Hentie's cheerful voice cut through my thoughts.

"Good morning, Hentie. I was wondering where you were."

"Did you want to talk to me about something?" She gave me a wriggle of her eyebrows. She couldn't have been more obvious if she tried, but it made me laugh anyway. I genuinely liked this woman.

"I do," I said. "Do you want to take a walk while we talk?"

"Lekker," she said. "That means nice or yummy in Afrikaans." And then she let Barkington down. He trotted over to me, sniffed my shoes and wagged his tail.

I bent and petted him for a bit while Hentie got a colorful glittery purple lead for her dog and clipped it onto his collar.

"Ready," she said.

Off we went, strolling down the deck together. It would have been pleasant if I didn't have a serious topic to talk to her about.

Hentie had chosen a cream pants suit today and matched it with another of her floral t-shirts and a scarf that she'd tied around her neck, along with a broad floppy sun hat that wobbled when she walked. "What a nice day," she said. "Not too hot, not too cold."

Barkington barked his agreement.

"Hentie," I said. "Tell me something."

"What do you wanna know?"

"I want to know if you heard any rumors about Angela," I said. "Any plots."

Hentie stopped walking and stared at me. "Plots?"

"Plans. Pranks, even."

She pressed her lips to one side and considered it. "What did you find out?"

I folded my arms.

"Oh come on, April. Surely, you've got to trust me a

little bit by now. I've been open with you about everything that's happened."

I didn't say anything.

"Listen, we can stand here all day, but we're going to have to talk about it at some point."

"Talk about what?"

"Your trust issues."

"This is going in a direction I didn't anticipate," I said, and started walking again.

Hentie fell into step beside me, shaking her head so that her floppy hat bobbled. "Name one thing I've done that you don't trust."

"You weren't upfront with me about what happened between Jocelyn and Angela."

"Ja, but that's different."

"How?"

Hentie stopped again and blew out a breath. "Because I was embarrassed about it. Wouldn't you be? Angela took advantage of my friend, and I let it happen."

"It's not your fault she did that."

"If you say so."

We continued our tour around the VIP deck, and I worked it over in my mind.

"Fine, you don't have to trust me," Hentie said. "But I can't answer your questions about plots and plans, if you don't give me something more. What kind of plot? Or plan?"

"It's come to my attention," I said, lowering my voice. "That Calliope and her friends may or may not have been interested in pranking Angela. I want to find out what type of prank they played and if you knew about it." And that had taken a lot for me to say. If I couldn't trust Hentie... Well, then I'd have to kill her.

That was a joke.

The only reason I'd have to kill someone was if they directly threatened my country or the NSIB.

"A prank by Calliope." Hentie picked up Barkington. "I wouldn't put it past her. She likes to cause trouble. And Betty will do whatever she says. She's basically her right hand."

"And Eve?"

"Eve's involved too? The performer?"

"Yeah," I said.

"No, I haven't heard anything about a prank. If Calliope wanted to involve me, she would have, but she didn't. Sorry, April. I wish I could help."

"That's fine. It's not your fault. Apparently, Calliope believed you were close with Angela."

Hentie rolled her eyes. "Of course she did. Calliope thinks everyone's conspiring against her."

"Do you—?"

A shriek cut across my words, and Hentie and I exchanged a wide-eyed glance.

"What was that?" Hentie hissed.

I scanned the pool deck down below. Another feral cry sounded, and then Calliope appeared, running between the deck chairs, vaulting over them, and screaming her head off, her floaty cotton dress streaming behind her.

"Wat op aarde?" Hentie grasped the railing with one hand, the other holding Barkington away from the fray, as if to shield him from the strangeness of the scene.

"Why is she running?"

The question had just left my mouth when the reason presented itself. Detective White, followed by two other police officers, both of them huffing and puffing and red-cheeked, darted after Calliope.

"Stop!" Detective White screamed. "Stop right there."

One of the police officers removed a Taser from his belt as he ran.

"Uh oh," I said.

"They won't do that, surely? She's in her sixties. That can't be good for the heart," Hentie said.

Calliope reached the railing and clattered against it. She tried to run off to the left, into the ship itself, but a police officer blocked her path. She turned, and the second officer stepped in her way.

"Leave me alone," she yelled.

The other guests stared and gossiped behind their hands. A few mothers were trying to shield their children.

Detective White approached Calliope, his hands out, as if he was calming an animal rather than talking to a woman. And then it happened. The officers closed in, and Calliope Benson was slapped in cuffs.

<h1 style="text-align:center">Twenty-One</h1>

"THAT WAS *SOMETHING*." HENTIE WAS WIDE-eyed as Calliope was led away by the police.

I took a mental image. Of the way Detective White looked up at the deck above, scanning it, looking for what?

Or for whom?

"They must have evidence against her. I wonder how they got it and what it was," I mused.

"It's probably got to do with that prank you told me about," Hentie said instantly. "The prank that you said Calliope was going to pull on Angela. What if it led to her death?"

"I'll have to find out—"

Sharp footsteps on the deck interrupted me, and I cut the conversation off. Hentie stiffened, and Barkington let out a volley of yaps and barks as Captain Quinton rounded the corner. He was pristine in his white uniform, the navy strips on his shoulders marked with gold stripes, his captain's hat placed neatly on his head.

"What's going on?" he asked, his tone clipped.

"Good morning, Captain Quinton," Hentie said, with a timid smile. She shuffled away from him, shushing Barkington, even though he wouldn't stop barking.

He didn't like the captain one bit, and I didn't blame the Chihuahua for it. The captain was all kinds of repressed. Just the way he moved told me he had a giant carrot where the sun didn't shine.

"Captain Quinton," I said. "Nice to see you."

He frowned at me, sweeping his gaze over my plain white tennis shoes, my jeans and blouse, up to my eyes. "You're not a VIP passenger."

"I'm not," I said. "I was the contractor who served ice cream at your party."

"Ah. The dog rescuer." His gray eyebrow lifted. "And you're on the VIP deck because...?"

"She's my guest," Hentie said, choking it out.

"Yeah, that and you gave me a pass for the ship as part of my payment," I said. "If you recall, Captain Quinton?"

But he looked over my head, and I got the distinct impression that I'd been summarily dismissed. Too bad I wasn't the type of woman to be dismissed that easily.

"What happened?" Quinton asked. "I heard screams."

"Calliope Benson was arrested," I said.

Quinton's gaze met mine again. "Arrested. On board my ship?"

"Yeah. Right down there on the pool deck. In front of everyone," I said. "Detective White did the arresting, so you might want to call him. I don't know if the ship will be able to leave port today."

"Impossible," Quinton said. "Impossible. The ship will leave today."

"I'm sure Detective White will be in touch with you," I said.

Quinton gritted his teeth, the squeak and grind audible, and then he charged past me, walking like he owned the deck and everyone on it.

Hentie let out a breath. "You've got a death wish," she said. "I've never seen anyone stand up to him like that before."

"Stand up to him? That's what's passing as standing up to someone nowadays?" I watched the captain's retreating back, my eyes narrowed. "He's got an elevated opinion of himself, and he's—" I didn't want to echo Jayce's words from last night, so I let it be. "Looks like the ship can't leave after all."

But why had they arrested Calliope? They must have evidence. Reasonable suspicion.

"Nobody talks back to the captain," Hentie said. "Staff

get fired if they do, and passengers, well, he's very good at making people feel awkward or afraid."

"So, he's a bully," I said.

"Definitief," Hentie said. "That's definitely in English. He's scary."

"He's a man who lets power get to his head. And he can't do anything to you, Hentie. You paid for your ticket. The most he can do is rescind my pass to be on board the ship, and if he does that well, so be it." I had other means of getting on board.

Barkington trembled in Hentie's arms, and she stroked his head.

We lingered on the deck for a few minutes before finally setting off back down it, following the captain's steps. Neither of us talked, but I got the feeling Hentie was as curious about what had happened as I was. The man was furious at Detective White. He wanted the ship to set sail. He wasn't concerned about Angela at all, only about himself.

Could Jayce have been onto something?

By the time we reached the broad open area where Captain Quinton had hosted his VIP birthday party, we'd lost sight of him. Doubtless, the man had charged off the ship to confront Detective White and save Calliope. The latter only because it would help Quinton leave port.

"The smells from the kitchen are making me hungry

all over again," Hentie said. "They know how to cook on board this ship. I wish—"

The doors that led into the kitchen swung open and a man in chef's whites strode out onto the deck. He swore profusely, focused on the phone in his hand.

Hentie pulled a face.

"The darn idiot," the chef said, then lifted the phone to his ear. "Jayce, where are you? You can't pull a stunt like this. I warned you after the last time that there would be consequences for this type of behavior." The chef, he had a round face that was red and streaked with sweat, spotted us. He cleared his throat. "Call me when you get this message." He hung up and stowed his phone in his pocket. "Sorry, ladies, I didn't mean to interrupt your morning walk." And then he turned to leave.

"Wait," I said.

The chef faced me. "Can I help you with something, ma'am?"

"You mentioned Jayce," I said. "The sous chef?"

He frowned. "You know him?" The chef's gaze swept over me, taking in my clothes, and then moved to Hentie. "You're not a VIP passenger?"

"No," I said, and released Hentie's arm. I walked over to the chef. "What's your name?"

"Kevin," he said. "I'm the head chef for the VIP kitchens. You know Jayce?"

"I know him," I replied. "He came by my guesthouse last night spouting all kinds of rumors about the captain and his new girlfriend."

"Captain Quinton doesn't have a girlfriend," Kevin murmured. "Idiot. What does he think he's doing, spreading rumors like that? I knew he wasn't stable. I told them not to hire him, and now we all have to pay the price."

"What's going on? He didn't turn up for work?" I asked.

"No, he didn't. And I have an entire lunch to make without a sous chef as a result," Kevin said. "I swear, I'm going to throttle him the minute I find him."

I moved past Kevin toward the kitchen doors.

"Hey, wait, what are you doing?"

I entered the kitchen and was surrounded by delicious smells and the sounds of the chef's cooking, calling out to each other, as they prepared everything for lunch. I walked to the freezer.

Kevin chased after me. "What on earth are you doing? Stop. You're not allowed in here." He grabbed hold of my arm, and I pinched him beneath the elbow. He released me instantly. "What the—?"

I reached the freezer and unlocked it, then swung the door wide.

But the space inside was empty of dead bodies or any evidence of Jayce.

"What are you doing, lady?"

"Just checking," I said. "Have you reported your sous chef missing?"

"No, why would I—?"

"I suggest you do." And then I left him standing there, wide-eyed.

Twenty-Two

It was about time I did this.

Hentie kept her arm looped in mine as I walked back toward the VIP rooms. "You're sure you want to do this?" she asked.

"Positive."

Barkington yapped, and Hentie stroked him, smiling softly to herself. "There, there, poepie. It's okay."

"Poepie?"

"It's a term of endearment," Hentie said. "I'm calling him a little fart, I guess you could say."

"And that's a term of endearment?" I laughed.

"It is for me," Hentie said.

We rounded a corner, heading down a cream-carpeted hallway with matching walls and gold jacquard overlay.

Under different circumstances, I would have asked Hentie to let me do this on my own, but she was the perfect cover. And I'd be interested to see how she interacted during our "mission."

"There," Hentie said, nodding toward a door on our left. "That's Betty's room."

We stopped in front of it, and I knocked.

A moment later, it opened, and Betty appeared. Her eyes were owlish, just as they'd been before, but this time, there were dark circles underneath them. She clasped a scrunched up tissue in one hand, the other grasping the side of the door so that the tips of her fingers turned white.

"Y-Yes?" She swallowed, her voice raspy and soft. "What did you w-want?"

"To talk to you, of course," Hentie said, and Barkington backed her up with another bark.

"How are you feeling, Betty?" I asked. "Is this a bad time?"

"It's... yes, I guess you could—"

"Calliope was arrested," Hentie said.

Betty flinched. "I— Yes."

"But you already knew that," I guessed.

Betty's shoulders slumped. "Oh, it's awful. I feel awful. I'm a terrible, terrible person. And then she burst into tears."

Immediately, Hentie swept into the room, and I followed suit. I wrapped an arm around Betty's shoulders. "There, there," I said. "It's all right. This must be so difficult for you, but it's going to be okay."

"It's never going to be okay, ever again," Betty howled.

Barkington took his cue from her and let out a tiny doggy howl of his own. Hentie cooed at him and stroked his head.

I kicked the door shut with my heel and walked Betty through to her plush leather sofa. I sat her down on it, then gestured to Hentie. "Would you mind making us something to drink?"

"I'm on it," she said, and let Barkington down. He trailed his lead as he ran toward me and barked to be helped up.

I lifted him into my lap, and he licked my fingers as thanks for the attention. "What's going on, Betty? Why do you feel so guilty? It's not your fault that Calliope was arrested."

"Those police probably know what they're doing," Hentie said, as she fixed the coffee. "Listen, you should consider yourself lucky. Where I come from, you'd be lucky if the police even showed up in an emergency."

"R-Really?" Betty asked.

"Ja," Hentie hissed, pulling a face. "Listen, I once had some guys who tried to break into my house, but when I called the cops, they only got there like an hour later. The alarm company people got there before them."

I bit back my humor, not at the horrible situation Hentie had described, but just the way she interacted with the world. She was so blunt and open, and I couldn't help liking her for it.

"Betty," I said, patting her back. "What happened?"

"I—I—" She sniffled and dabbed the end of her nose. "I was the one who made the police think that they should talk to Calliope."

"Talk to her?" Hentie asked. "You mean arrest her?"

"Yes." Another wail.

And another bout of howling from the Chihuahua in my lap. I covered his little ears in case that was what was getting to him, but he wagged his tail at me, unconcerned.

Hentie came over with a mug of coffee for Betty.

A few sips seemed to help her calm down, and, finally, Betty turned toward me, her eyes watery with her guilt. "A few days ago," she said, "Detective White came to see me."

"What did he say?" I asked, and accepted a mug from Hentie, nodding my thanks.

Hentie settled down on a leather armchair across from us, placing her cup on the coffee table. She tapped her fingers on the arms of the chair, watching, but occasionally casting her gaze to the view of the deck and the ocean.

"He said that he was still investigating what had

happened to Angela," Betty whispered. "That he was questioning people, but that I had to keep it a secret from everyone on board the ship. He said that if I told others about this, Captain Quinton might hear."

"He was worried about Captain Quinton?"

"Yeah," Betty said. "He mentioned that the captain wanted the ship to leave, but that he couldn't allow that to happen. Not when there was a murder to be investigated."

So he had told Quinton what he wanted to hear. He had given himself a timeline to solve the murder, and he was close. He had to be if he'd made an arrest.

"What did he ask you about Calliope?"

Hentie leaned forward, her green eyes wide and glittering.

Betty gulped. "A lot of things. He asked me if she would stand to gain from Angela's passing, and I told him about her brother's stipulation that if he should die, and Angela should die, all of his assets would pass to his Calliope. They were very close growing up. Thick as thieves."

"That's information that he could've gotten anywhere," I said. "You shouldn't feel guilty about that."

"There were other things he asked me."

I waited.

Betty's bottom lip trembled. "He wanted to know about... about if Calliope wanted to harm Angela."

"And did she?"

"N-No," she said. "I don't think so. But I— I didn't know all the details."

"Of what?" I asked.

"She was planning something with Eve." Betty dabbed her nose furiously and squished the tissue into her hand. "And she wanted me to be involved."

"What did she say?" I asked.

"She didn't tell me much," Betty said, "because I didn't want her to. I asked her not to tell me the minute she said that she was planning something mean."

"Those were the words she used?" I asked. "Mean?"

"Yeah. She said that Angela deserved what was coming to her, that she had had enough, and that it was time to teach her a lesson, and that Eve agreed."

"Why would Eve agree?" I asked.

"Because she hated Angela as much as anybody else. Angela tried to get her fired from her job. She kept reporting Eve for inappropriate behavior and fraternization to the point where poor Eve didn't know whether the captain would keep her on board or not," Betty said. "They both hated Angela, and I didn't like her either, but I didn't want to be a part of something like that. It felt wrong." She sniffed. "But now Detective White thinks that Calliope has done this, and I can't... There's no way she would kill her. There's no way."

I patted Betty on the back and met Hentie's gaze. She pursed her lips and gave a nod.

Anyone was capable of murder. And now, Eve had a motive.

Twenty-Three

"Nice to see you," Eve said. "Though, I wasn't expecting any visitors." The pretty young performer wore her hair in curlers and held a cigarette in one hand. She lived in the staff quarters on the lower decks, which meant I'd left Hentie in the VIP section and come alone.

It was one thing for me to wander around on board the ship and go where I wanted, but Hentie would look out of place below deck.

"Nice to see you too, Eve," I said. "I wanted to talk to you and see how you were holding up."

"Come on in," Eve said, and opened the door. "Don't worry about the covered cases." She pointed to glass cages with fabric draped over their sides. "Some of my snakes are aggressive, so I keep them in the dark during the day. The rattlesnake for instance. You can't let him see you or he'll lunge at the glass and injure himself."

"Of course," I said, and followed her inside.

Her quarters were tiny. There was a bed, a table, and enough space for the snakes and that was about it. The ensuite was a shower with a toilet right beside it.

Eve wore slippers that flopped as she walked. She opened her tiny porthole window and blew a puff of smoke out of it. "Not what you expected, is it?" she asked. "Granted, you've been hanging out with the VIPs. I've seen how they live. Grand suites while the staff members live in tiny rooms like this. Believe it or not, my room is one of the biggest. The other girls all share rooms. They have to. There's not enough space for all the crew other-wise, and it's not like we're on the cruise."

I sat down on a rickety armchair beside the bathroom door.

"I'd offer you coffee but I'm fresh out," she said, gesturing to her pot. It had a crack near the lip. Another puff of smoke out of the window. "So, you wanted to check on me. About what?"

"You haven't heard?"

Eve shook her head and dropped some ash out of the window.

"Calliope was arrested."

Eve's eyelashes fluttered. "What?"

"She was arrested. I didn't hear the charges, but it's probably in connection to what happened to Angela."

"But I thought they ruled that as an accident." Eve had forgotten her cigarette. It smoked between her fingers. She shook her head. "This is— That's just crazy. Calliope isn't capable of murder."

"Detective White thinks she is," I said. "That's why I came to see you. I thought you might be able to help me."

"Help you how?" She held the cigarette up to her lips and took a drag, her hand trembling. "With what?" The ash dropped onto her chest and she swept it away with a grimace.

I took a mental image of her, standing there among the snakes, for later dissection.

"Well, the police seem to think that Calliope murdered Angela as a part of some prank she had planned," I said. "I wanted to find out what the prank was. Maybe, if I know that, I can prove her innocence."

"Prank?"

I nodded, assessing the way she acted. The slight flickers of emotion that crossed her face. Disbelief, fear, anger. Disbelief.

Interesting.

"Yeah, apparently you and Calliope were planning to get Angela back somehow? Betty mentioned it to the police and this seems to have sparked the arrest."

"That's... Wow, Betty said that to them?" Eve asked. "I would have expected her to be a little more loyal." She dropped the stub of her cigarette into an empty coffee mug. "That's crazy that she would tell them something like that since she was the one who hated Angela the most. And who was involved in the prank."

"What *was* the prank?"

"It was harmless. We slipped a fake spider onto her pillow," Eve said, rolling her eyes. "It wasn't even a real spider. It's not like that could have killed her." She shook her head rapidly. "No, this is ridiculous. Impossible. That Betty is behind this."

"You think Betty's the killer?"

Eve gnawed on the corner of her lip. "I don't know. I don't know if she's the murderer, but she's definitely got some motive for trying to get Calliope arrested. Probably jealousy. You know Angela used to report me to the captain all the time. She used to accuse me of fraternization. I almost got fired." She pointed at her chest. "But the police already talked to me about that, and they cleared me. They cleared Calliope too. No, no. This must be about something else. Or there must be another reason."

Eve returned to the porthole window and stared out, shaking her head.

"Another reason?"

"Yeah, if Calliope really did this, I had nothing to do

with it, and Detective White knows that." She sucked in a breath. "This is bad. This is really bad. I could lose my job over this, and I haven't even done anything wrong. They can't seriously think that I had anything to do with it."

"I thought you said Detective White cleared you."

"He did."

"Then you have nothing to worry about."

Eve exhaled. "You're right. It's just shocking, that's all. I didn't think Calliope was capable of something like that. She's soft. Not really well-traveled. She barely knows how to stand up for herself. She wouldn't say anything to Angela when she used to pick on her."

I nodded. "There are all kinds in the world," I said. "So you have no idea what this could be about?"

"No," Eve said. "No. I don't think it's got anything to do with a silly prank or a fake spider. It's got to be about something else."

She fell silent, staring out of the window and clearly lost in thought.

"Eve," I said. "Have you seen Jayce recently?"

Her blue-eyed gaze snapped to mine instantly. "Jayce?"

"Yeah. He's not around. They're looking for him in the kitchens."

"You seem to know a lot about what happens on this ship."

I met her stare for stare, wordless, and let a slow smile

spread across my face. "You would be correct in that presumption."

She swallowed. "I don't know where Jayce is, and I don't care. He's my ex-boyfriend. I don't ever want to see him again."

"Did he do something that bad?"

"He's crazy. He accused me of murdering a man, and said the captain was in on it too. Out of his mind," Eve said.

"He also seems to think that you and Captain Quinton are dating."

Eve gasped. "The scandal that would cause." She laughed. "No, we're not dating. Sure, Quinton's handsome, but he's also incredibly overbearing and arrogant. I wouldn't want a man like that sharing my life with me." She gestured to the room. "Besides, look at me. I'm a lowly entertainer and the captain is... well, the captain." The last part came out sour.

"I'm going to try to figure this out," I said. "This must be difficult for you."

"Calliope doesn't deserve to be behind bars. She hasn't done anything wrong," Eve said. "Ugh. Trust me to always make friends who disappear." She laughed. "It's my lot in life, I guess. I always manage to lose the people I care about. It's a tragedy."

I excused myself from Eve's room with a nod and a

smile, but the minute I stepped into the hall, it disappeared.

A passing crew member nodded to me, and kept on moving, calling out to a woman near the end of the hall. "Did you hear? We're leaving tonight?"

"I thought the detective said we couldn't leave."

"Captain's going to do it anyway."

I started walking before I broke into a run.

Twenty-Four

THE CAPTAIN'S QUARTERS WERE ON THE TOP deck. I reached them out of breath, my mind burning with questions. The image of Eve, standing between her snake cages, curlers in her hair, had taken its place on the cork-board, a thin red line connecting it to the others, and strangely to that fuzzy picture.

What was that picture? It was slightly clearer.

There was a blue background, that was for sure, a splash of white, and of deep brown, but what was it?

I frowned and knocked on the door to Captain Quinton's quarters.

The door swung open abruptly, and I feigned a small fright. It was the "normal" reaction, and I didn't want to blow my cover. Thankfully, the detective hadn't looked into my past too much or I'd have been on my way out of town by now.

"What do you want?" Quinton sneered.

The handsome facade dropped, and he was purely full of rage.

"Captain Quinton," I said. "Sorry to bug you, but we need to talk."

"We really don't."

"Oh, but we do," I said. "It's about Detective White. I think he's got this all wrong."

"What?" Quinton's anger faded a little.

"I don't understand why on earth he would arrest Calliope. I mean, it's ridiculous. She's an upstanding VIP passenger, and she didn't touch Angela. You know, I was there that night, right behind the ice cream bar. I saw *everything.*"

Quinton's sharp steely eyes narrowed. He cleared his throat, clearing schooling himself to calm, then stepped back and nodded to me. "Would you like to come in for something to drink?"

"That's so kind of you, Captain," I said, and entered his quarters.

They were much fancier than the quarters of the crew members down below. He had a flat screen TV on the wall, and a living room suite, a gorgeous view of the ocean, and of course, a large comfortable bedroom, glimpsed through the open doorway, with white sheets on the bed.

It wasn't nearly as opulent as the luxury suites, but it was comfortable.

"Take a seat," he said, gesturing to a leather sofa pressed against the wall, across from the TV.

I smiled at him and sat down. "Thank you."

"Coffee, tea? Something stronger?" His sly smile made my skin crawl.

I giggled and covered my mouth. "At this time of the morning?" I asked. "I couldn't. I would love some soda if you have it."

"Sure," he said, and headed for the mini-fridge. He returned with a can of Coke and handed it to me, then walked off to get his own.

Swiftly, I checked for cameras then removed a wet wipe from my pocket. I shed its packaging then wiped the top of the soda can and popped the tab.

By the time the captain returned, I was sipping from the can with a smile. "Thank you," I said. "It's a hot day and that makes this extra refreshing." Why was the captain worried about what I had seen unless he had something to hide?

He took a seat on the armchair across from mine, holding a tumbler of brown fluid. He took a sip from it.

"Bourbon," he said. "One of my favorites. Sure I can't interest you?"

"Oh, no thank you, Captain. I'm not much of a drinker. But I appreciate the coke." I took a sip from the can, watching as he assessed me.

He couldn't spike a sealed can, but he could have laced the rim with something, hence the wet wipe.

I gave him a broad smile. "Is everything okay?" I asked.

Captain Quinton frowned, looking from the can to my face and back again. "Yeah, fine. You mentioned you saw something on the night of Angela's unfortunate passing."

"I saw everything. I saw that she took a bite of ice cream and that she fell over. And I know that she had plenty of enemies."

"Hmm."

"Including Calliope, but that doesn't mean she killed her."

"No, it doesn't," Captain Quinton said, still studying me like I was a rubix cube he couldn't solve.

"And Hentie didn't like her either. Betty too," I said. "And then there's Eve."

A slight stiffening of the shoulders, a sudden freeze to the captain's expression.

Jackpot.

"Eve despised her, I hear."

"I don't see how that's possible," Captain Quinton said. "They never interacted."

"They didn't?" I asked. "I thought they were friends. I mean, that's the impression I got when I saw them hanging out the other day."

Captain Quinton swirled the tumbler of fluid, effecting a casual lean in his armchair, crossing one leg over the other. "You're mistaken."

"I don't think I am, Captain," I said, breathlessly. "I saw them together. They were having fun, although Eve was a little under the weather. She said it was an allergy, but I doubt it was that."

"You think there was another reason she was sick?"

"Oh, sure. The common cold." Or something else. Something more sinister than he knew all about. "I just want the ship to set sail again, don't you?"

"Why do you want the ship to set sail?" Quinton asked.

"Think about it, Captain. The minute the ship sets sail, Carmel Springs can get back to being Carmel Springs. The Emerald Countess has made the lives of the locals very uncomfortable. It's not just the fact that it's an eyesore," I said, "but that now it's the sight of a murder."

"Excuse me?" Captain Quinton leaned forward. "A murder?"

"Yeah," I said.

Interesting that he didn't care I'd called it an eyesore.

"It's *not* a murder. This was a terrible accident," Captain Quinton said.

"If that's true, Captain, then why did they arrest Calliope?"

"That is something I'm going to figure out." He glared off to one side, the cogs clearly working in his mind.

"Captain," I said. "Do you know your sous chef is missing?"

"What?" He speared me with another aggressive gaze.

"Your sous chef, Jayce?" I shook my head and placed my fingers against my lips. "He's missing. Kevin, your chef from the VIP kitchens, was frustrated about it this morning. Do you know where he is?"

"What's that got to do with anything?" Quinton rose from his seat. "Look, this visit was... pleasant, but I think it's time for you to go."

"Of course. I wouldn't want to outstay my welcome." I got up, placing the soda can on the table in front of me.

Quinton glanced at it again.

"Have a good day, Captain."

He grunted and walked me to the door. I stepped out onto the deck, and the minute I was out of his cabin, he slapped the door shut behind me.

The man was dangerous. And Jayce had been right. He was hiding something, because Captain Quinton wasn't interested in defending the ship. He was interested in defending himself. He wasn't bothered by my opinion of The Emerald Countess, only that there had been a murder on board.

Either that was because he was guilty, or it was because he had something else to hide, and I was going to find out what that was. Tonight.

Twenty-Five

"Thanks for the invite," I murmured, taking my place at the table beside Hentie. Barkington sat in her lap, peering over the table at everyone at our small dining table. There were a few other diners, but they mostly chatted among themselves.

Betty remained at the table nearest the front, though her eyes were red-rimmed, and she was alone. The news about her potential involvement in Angela's death had spread through the cruise ship quick as lightning.

"Ja, well, you told me you needed a way in, and I'm happy to help," Hentie said.

I squeezed my friend's arm.

"Do you think he's going to go ahead with it?" Hentie asked. "You know, setting sail."

"If he's going to do it, it will be tonight. You're sure he dines with the VIP passengers most nights?"

Hentie nodded. "He likes to be the center of attention, so trust me, he's gonna be here." She made a face. "I don't like it, the way he interacts with people. He puts up such a front, and then when you do something wrong, he lets you know in his way."

I settled back in my chair.

The meal tonight was delicious and I was seriously lucky to be here. It was the second time I'd eaten the food prepared by the VIP kitchen, and probably the last, so I enjoyed every bite. Lobster thermidor, and mini-lasagnas, salads that tasted better than anything green I'd ever eaten, and the best wines or juices or milkshakes.

Captain Quinton arrived during the performance by the aerial artist. He took a seat at Betty's table, and the minute he'd done that, others started to join him. Betty perked up a bit and talked to him, smiling as she picked at her food.

Wine was poured and the party was already in full swing by the time Eve took to the stage.

A hush went over the group as she appeared with the first of her snakes.

"She's amazing with them," Hentie said. "Scary. There are all kinds of snakes under her spell. I don't know how she does it."

Eve wore a skin-tight outfit today, glittering beneath the lights on the stage, and she turned this way and that, showing off the massive python draped over her arms.

"And that's the reason I keep a close eye on Barkington," Hentie said. "Ja jong, those snakes have escaped before, and the last thing I need is for one of those massive things to eat my puppy dog."

"They've escaped before?"

Hentie nodded. "Apparently before I boarded the ship there was an emergency, but I don't know much of the details."

The fuzzy image on my corkboard swam into view. Clearer than before. What was it?

Was that the pool deck?

Eve danced with the snake to music, then brought out a wicker basket on stage. The music dulled, and she deposited the python into the waiting hands of an assistant.

She spread her arms in front of the crowd. "Ladies and gentlemen," she said. "Thank you for attending my show this evening. Of course, it's a happy accident that we're serving dinner at exactly the same time, isn't it?" She tittered a laugh.

The guests laughed and clapped.

Captain Quinton stared at her, his gaze dark.

Dark and... there was something else there.

A waitress, one I recognized as my helper from the beginning of the week, passed by our table and I grabbed hold of her arm. "Tessa," I said. "Hi."

"Oh, hey, the ice cream lady. Are you good? Do you need a refill on anything?" she asked, with a quick smile.

"Is the sous chef in the kitchen?" I asked.

"Who, Jayce?" Tessa gave an uneasy glance toward the table where Captain Quinton sat watching the show. "No. Nobody's seen him since this morning."

I nodded. "Thanks. Another strawberry milkshake?"

"I'll get that for you." And then she swept off again.

I'd tried to visit Jayce at his quarters after my talk with the captain, but he wasn't around, and his roommate had no idea what had happened to him. I'd visited right away and asked Hentie for the invitation because I got the sense that I wouldn't be welcome on board the ship for much longer. Captain Quinton didn't like me, and I had his attention now.

I watched the side of his face while he admired Eve on stage.

"I have a special surprise for you this evening," Eve said, turning in a grand sweeping circle and striking a pose. "You see, every night, I bring out my pythons, I show you the rattlesnake, and the iguanas, but tonight, I have a treat. A snake that will thrill and excite. So deadly that you'll be terrified of what it can do to you."

Shivers ran through the room. A palpable air of tension building up to a feverish point.

"Tonight, I have a foreign and exotic snake for your examination," Eve said. "For your pleasure." And then she removed the lid of the basket and peered inside. "When I tell you that this snake is the most deadly creature you will ever lay eyes on, I'm not lying. Prepare yourself."

Eve reached into the basket and removed a long, green snake with jewel-like black eyes. I'd never seen anything like it. It was a snake, but those eyes… They were deadly. Its scales were a darker shade of green, the bottom of its thin, sinuous body, an almost lime green.

Hentie gasped beside me.

"What?" I murmured.

"It's a boomslang," she whispered.

"This is the South African boomslang," Eve said, with a completely different accent to the one Hentie had used. "And one bite is so venomous, it will kill you where you stand."

"Not technically true," Hentie muttered. "I grew up on a farm in the Western Cape and there were plenty of them around. They're not that aggressive, and if they bite you, the bite is fatal if you don't get anti-venom, but it takes days before it will kill you."

My vision narrowed to almost a pinpoint, and my

mind took a snapshot of Eve in her glittery green costume, holding the boomslang aloft.

"Say that again," I whispered.

"Which part?"

"How long does it take to kill you?"

"Days," Hentie whispered, while Eve trotted back and forth on the stage, flaunting the snake. "That's what's dangerous about them. They can bite you and the symptoms aren't that shocking until you're dead."

"What are the symptoms?"

"Oh, nausea and vomiting. You'll get headaches. Of course, the snake bite can get swollen and itchy, but if—"

I laid my hand on Hentie's arm and squeezed it.

"April? What's wrong?"

Barkington let out a tiny bark and peered up at me.

"I have to go," I whispered. "Now. I need you to cover for me, all right?"

"Do you want me to come with you?"

"No," I said. "I need you to stall the captain and Eve. Make sure neither of them leave this room, all right? Not for at least a half an hour after the show is done."

"Okay, I've got your back, Jack," Hentie said, with a firm nod.

I excused myself from the table and headed for the side door, walking casually and acting as if I was on my phone, texting someone. Really, that fuzzy image in my mind was clear.

The image, the snapshot that had been hidden from my eyes, was the picture of Angela, the victim, standing beside the deck chairs, scratching her leg.

Twenty-Six

I MOVED THROUGH THE HALLS LIKE A SHADOW, past crew members or passengers, smiling at anyone who looked my way and acting as if I wasn't in a rush to get where I was going. Hentie had my number, and I sent her a text as I wound my way toward the elevator.

> Any news?

> She's still on the stage charming people and snakes. But what's the difference when it comes to the captain, eh? LOL.

> And he's still in his seat?

> Yes. Will text the minute they leave.

> Thank you.

I reached the elevator and took it down to the crew quarters. I exited into the hallway and walked down it casually, again, pretending I was on my phone until I reached the camera that kept watch on the hall. I snapped on my latex gloves, disabled the camera as I'd done with the one outside Calliope's room, then picked the lock to Eve's room and let myself in.

The space smelled of snakes, but the tanks were all empty. I clicked on the lights and started my search.

The room was much smaller than any of the suites I'd been in before, which meant it was easier to search. I rifled through the closet, checked the bathroom, and under the bed. The nightstand drawer held a weathered copy of *Wuthering Heights* and a cellphone.

Her cellphone.

Of course.

She wouldn't be able to take it with her on stage.

I brought my phone out of my pocket and made quick work of hacking into hers. The password was a code, 5627, and I input it into the device. It unlocked, and I searched through her messages immediately.

QUINTON

They're onto us.

Would you relax? Nothing bad is going to happen. It's not a big deal, okay, nobody's going to realize what's going on.

I would love to relax, Eve, but given that you've made it very difficult to do so, I can't. This is all your fault.

I got away with the last one, didn't I? And you helped me. You owe me. You can't back out now.

I wish we'd never met.

Yeah, well, that's your problem. Look Quinty, you're stuck with me.

Don't call me that!

You're my brother. You owe me this much, do you understand? You owe me for everything I've done to protect you.

I'm doing everything I can.

Do more. I need you to deal with Jayce. He's been going around spreading rumors about us. The fool thinks we're dating.

What do you mean, deal with him? What do you expect me to do?

What's necessary. Lock him up until I can deal with him.

I took pictures of the texts then returned the phone to where I'd found it. Quinton and Eve were siblings? And they were working together to cover up these murders? Why? The guy who had died, the previous sous chef, he'd been one of Eve's victims.

And her name wasn't a real name. It was just her stage name.

She hadn't even been a suspect until now.

Jayce was in danger. I had to put a stop to this now before it was too late. I turned and ran from the room.

THE CAPTAIN'S QUARTERS WERE LOCKED, BUT I used my lockpick set to get in, heedless of the camera outside. I wanted the security on board to see me. It would cause a fuss and bring them to the scene, and it would stop the ship from leaving.

I burst into the suite and a muffled thump came from the captain's bedroom.

I rushed past the living room and into the bedroom.

Jayce lay on the floor, his hands tied behind his back.

He'd clearly fallen off a chair near the end of the bed and had tried to work his way to the door.

I slipped my knife out of the pocket of my jeans and cut him free, then ripped the tape off his mouth.

Jayce yelled in pain. "Quick," he whispered. "You have to get out of here. Save yourself. They'll come back. They will—"

"Calm down," I said. "They're not coming back. But security will be here any second, and so will the cops." Because I had Detective White's number thanks to that card he'd given me earlier in the week. I helped Jayce upright and to his feet. He was woozy as if he'd been drugged.

The phone rang in my ear, and finally clicked.

"Hello?" Detective White's voice was stern. "Who is this?"

"This is April Waters," I said. "I'm in Captain Quinton's cabin. He kidnapped a man and has helped his sister, Eve, murder Angela and another man by snake bite or venom. I need you to come out here, immediately."

There was silence on the other end of the line. "Get out of there. Get that man to safety. I'm on my way, all right? I'm on my way!" And then he hung up.

I helped Jayce out of the room and onto the deck, just as security rounded the corner, followed by a man wearing a captain's hat. The co-captain was my guess. He was young, with a strong jawline and a pronounced dark brow.

"Stop right there!" One of the guards streaked toward us.

I stopped, helping Jayce to a seat on the deck first, then turned toward the group of men, ready to spring to action now that the danger had passed. "The police are on their way." My phone blipped in my pocket several times.

"What's the meaning of this?" The co-captain frowned. "Who are you?"

"My name is April Waters," I said. "I serve ice cream on a silly food truck. My favorite color is blue. Are you satisfied now? Would you like to know what happened to your VIP sous chef?"

His gaze drifted down to Jayce. "Of course. What's going on?"

"He was attacked by Captain Quinton," I said. "At the request of his sister, Eve."

"The snake charmer?" A security guard scratched his head nearby.

Footsteps tapped along the wooden deck, and Captain Quinton himself rounded the corner, his expression grim, Eve following just behind him.

Both of them froze at the sight of Jayce on the deck, their eyes widening. Quinton put up his hands. And Eve turned and fled.

"Stop right there!" A guard shouted.

Quinton followed his sister, but neither of them made it far. The police had arrived, and they cut the pair off before they could make it off the ship.

I dropped onto my haunches beside Jayce. He gave me a woozy smile.

"You all right?" I asked.

"Been better."

"Thanks for the tip off," I whispered.

"Thanks for helping me not get killed."

"We'll call it even." I patted him on the shoulder and gave him a smile. The crowds had already started gathering on the deck below, witnessing the spectacular downfall of Captain Quinton, the tyrant, and the no-longer-mysterious snake charmer, Eve.

Twenty-Seven

One week later...

"DID YOU HEAR THE NEWS?" SAM ASKED, TAKING a seat across from me at my favorite spot in the Oceanside. She placed a copy of the local newspaper on the table and tapped it. "Our very own Detective White solved the case on board that cruise ship."

"Really? What was the deal?" Sam had no idea I was involved, other than the fact that I'd "heard a commotion in the captain's cabin and had gone in to find Jayce." I planned on keeping it that way. I'd managed to keep my picture out of the paper, had refused to comment on the events on board the ship, and had done my best to deflect questions when serving ice cream on the truck.

Sam flattened out the newspaper on the table. "Apparently, Captain Quinton was this Eve woman's brother. They were estranged, but she caught up with him on board the ship, and they became friends. She's a real narcissistic piece of work, judging by what's being said about her. Manipulated him into covering up the murders by telling him that he was involved and that if he said a word, they'd both lose everything."

I sipped my coffee and glanced out at the I Scream for Ice Cream truck, glistening and lovely shades of pink and blue outside. I'd taken it to the car wash yesterday.

"She's going away for the rest of her life," Sam said. "Used venom from this venomous boomslang snake and injected it into the poor victim while she was asleep."

"It's been a week, though. She hasn't been tried yet."

"No, but I've got a feeling about this," Sam said, conspiratorially. "Trust me, I've had my fair share of experience with these types of cases."

"Oh, you mean with the sleuths you met before? The traveling food truck ladies?"

"Ruby and Bee, yes," Sam said. "They were masters at solving these types of crimes. But boy, did they get into a lot of trouble for it. The cops didn't like them interfering one bit."

"I bet," I said. "I prefer to stay out of those types of things."

"But surely you're happy you heard Jayce calling for help inside the captain's quarters?"

"Definitely," I said. "It was pretty traumatic, but I'm really glad that he's okay." I set my coffee cup aside carefully and leaned in. "The truth is, I'm glad that ship set sail this morning, and I can get back to my normal life. I was curious about what happened, but I would never get actively involved, you know?"

"Of course." But I sensed a little disappointment from Sam. She brushed her fingers over her forehead then laughed and shook her head. "The peace and quiet is nice. I'm glad you'll get to experience all of Carmel Springs now that the cruise ship is gone."

"I am too. I can't wait to explore and meet more of the locals. I'm the mood for some normal—"

A loud series of bangs sounded from the front of the guesthouse, and Sam jolted in her seat. "What on earth—?"

We both turned and peered through the doorway that looked out on the reception area of the guesthouse and its polished walnut desk. The doors swing inward. A shadow fell across the wooden floor. A woman?

And then a tiny, yellow-white dog trotted into the front hall and let out a terrific yap.

I blinked. "Barkington?"

Trouble hissed and leaped off the chair, the fur on his spine standing on end.

Hentie stepped through the door, dragging a set of wheeled suitcases behind her, and Sam jumped up to help out.

I abandoned my coffee, walking toward the shivering Barkington, who studied Trouble with sheer terror. I swept him into my arms and kissed him on the head. "Hentie?"

My new friend flashed me a broad grin and smoothed a hand over the front of her cherry red pants suit. "I thought," she said, "that you might need some company. Barkington kept howling at me every night. I think he misses you."

"But the cruise ship? Your husband?" I wasn't stunned to silence often, but I was close to it because the last thing I'd expected was for Hentie to walk through the front doors of the Oceanside Guesthouse.

"Oh, he'll understand. He doesn't care where I vacation, as long as I don't break the bank too much," Hentie said. "Besides, I'm going to call him just now and tell him what's going on."

"Just now?"

"Ja, now now," she said, waving a hand.

Sam and I shared a confused glance.

"I'll explain it at some point," Hentie said, then popped her hip and placed a hand on it. "So, you got any room in this inn or what?"

"We've got room," Sam said. "We'd be happy to have you."

"Doesn't look like your cat shares the opinion." Hentie smiled at Trouble, who was still highly suspicious of Barkington. The Chihuahua cuddled closer to my chest, trembling all over.

"Oh, he'll get used to it. Don't worry." Sam wiped her hands off on her cute navy blue apron and circled the desk. She tapped away on the keys. "So, Miss...?"

"Mrs. Hentie Cooper," she said, with a big smile.

I smiled too. I couldn't help it. I'd honestly thought I'd never see her again, and while it was better not to get attached to people when you lived the kind of life I did, it was lovely that she was here. She was interesting and kind and a refreshing person.

Do not get attached.

The last time I had cared about a person, they had wound up dead, and I couldn't let Hentie suffer the same fate. Or anyone else for that matter.

"So, Mrs. Cooper, how long will you be staying at the Oceanside?" Sam asked.

Hentie wriggled her gray eyebrows at me. "Indefinitely," she said.

And I threw back my head and laughed. A belly laugh that brought a howl from Barkington and several excited licks. It was the first real laugh I'd had in months, and it felt good. Almost cathartic. Because not only was the case solved, but I had made a friend doing it. And I couldn't wait to find out what Hentie would get up to in Carmel Springs.

Just as long as there were no corpses involved.

Will Hentie cause trouble in Carmel Springs? How will Delta overcome her fear of getting attached to people when she's always under threat? And just who is Delta hiding from and why? Find out more in MINT FREEZE MURDER.

<h1 style="text-align:center">Craving More Cozy Mystery?</h1>

If you had fun with Delta Mission, you'll, love getting to know Charlie Mission and her butt-kicking grandmother, Georgina. You can read the first chapter of Charlie's story, *The Case of the Waffling Warrants,* below!

"Come in, Big G, come in." I spoke under my breath so that the flesh-colored microphone seated against my throat picked up my voice. "What is your status?"

My grandmother, Georgina—pet name Gamma, code name Big G—was out on a special operation. Reconnaissance at the newest guesthouse in our town, Gossip. The reason? First, she was an ex-spy, as was I, and second, the woman who'd opened the guesthouse was her mortal enemy and in direct competition with my grandmother's establishment, the Gossip Inn.

Who was this enemy, this bringer of potential financial doom?

A middle-aged woman with a penchant for wearing pashminas and annoying anyone who looked her way.

Jessie Belle-Blue.

It was rumored that even thinking the woman's name summoned a murder of crows.

"I repeat, Big G, what is your status?"

"I'm en route to the nest," my grandmother replied in my earpiece.

I let out a relieved sigh and exited my bedroom, heading downstairs to help with the breakfast service.

In the nine months since I had retired as a spy, life in Gossip had been normal. In the Gossip sense of the term. I'd expected that my job as a server, maid, and assistant would bring the usual level of "cat herding" inherent when working at the inn. Whether that involved tracking down runaway cats, literally, or providing a guest with a moist towelette after a fainting spell—tempers ran high in Gossip.

What was the reason for the craziness? Shoot, it had to be something in the water.

I took the main stairs two at a time and found my friend, the inn's chef, paging through her recipe book in the lime green kitchen. Lauren Harris wore her red hair in a French braid today, apron stretched over her pregnant belly.

"Morning," I said, "how are you today?"

"Madder than a fat cat on a diet." She slapped her recipe book closed and turned to me.

Uh oh. Looks like it's time for more cat herding.

"What's wrong?"

"My supplier is out of flour and sugar. Can you believe that?" Lauren huffed, smoothing her hands over her belly while the clock on the wall ticked away. Breakfast was in two hours and Lauren loved baking cupcakes as part of the meal.

"Do you have enough supplies to make cupcakes for this morning?"

"Yes. But just for today," Lauren replied. "The guests are going to love my new waffle cupcakes, and they'll be sore they can't get anymore after this batch is done. Why, I should go down there and wring Billy's neck for doing this to me. He knows I take an order of sugar and flour every week, and I get it at just above cost too. What's Georgina going to say?"

"Don't stress, Lauren," I said. "We'll figure it out."

"Right." She brightened a little. "I nearly forgot you're the one who "fixes" things around here." Lauren winked at me.

She was the only person in the entire town who knew that my grandmother and I had once been spies for the NSIB—the National Security Investigative Bureau. But the news that I had helped solve several murders had spread through town, and now, anybody and everybody with a problem would call me up asking for help. A lot of them offered me money. And I was selective about who I chose to help.

"I'll check it out for you if you'd like," I said. "The flour issue."

"Nah, that's OK. I'm sure Billy will get more stock this week. I'll lean on him until he squeals."

"Sounds like you've been picking up tips from Georgina."

Lauren giggled then returned to her super-secret recipe book—no one but she was allowed to touch it.

"What's on the menu this morning?" I asked.

Lauren was the boss in the kitchen—she told me what to do, and I followed her instructions precisely. If I did anything else, like trying to read the recipe for instance, the food would end up burned, missing ingredients or worse.

The only place I wasn't a "fixer" was in the Gossip Inn's kitchen.

"Bacon and eggs over easy, biscuits and gravy, waffle cupcakes and... oh, I can't make fresh baked bread, can I?"

"Tell her I'll bring some back with me from the

bakery." Gamma's voice startled me. Goodness, I'd forgotten about the earpiece—she could hear everything happening in the kitchen.

"I'll text Georgina and ask her to bring bread from the bakery."

"You're a lifesaver, Charlotte."

We set to work on the breakfast—it was 7:00 a.m. and we needed everything done within two hours—and fell into our easy rhythm of baking and cooking.

My grandmother entered the kitchen at around 8:30 a.m., dressed in a neat silk blouse and a pair of slacks rather than the black outfit she'd left in for her spy mission. Tall, willowy, and with neatly styled gray hair, Gamma had always reminded me of Helen Mirren playing the Queen.

"Good morning, ladies," she said, in her prim, British accent. "I bring bread and tidings."

"What did you find out?" I asked.

"No evidence of the supposed ghost tours," Gamma said.

We'd started hosting ghost tours at the inn recently, so of course Jessie Belle-Blue wanted to do the same. She was all about under-cutting us, but, thankfully, the Gossip Inn had a legacy and over 1,000 positive reviews on Trip-Advisor.

Breakfast time arrived, and the guests filled the quaint dining area with its glossy tables, creaking wooden floors, and egg yolk yellow walls. Chatter and laughter leaked through the swinging kitchen doors with their porthole windows.

"That's my cue," I said, dusting off my apron, and heading out into the dining room.

I picked up a pot of coffee from the sideboard where we kept the drinks station and started my rounds.

Most of the guests had gathered around a center table in the dining room, and bursts of laughter came from the group, accompanied by the occasional shout.

I elbowed my way past a couple of guests—nobody could accuse me of having great people skills—apologizing along the way until I reached the table. The last time something like this had happened, a murder had followed shortly afterward.

Not this time. No way.

"—the last thing she'd ever hear!" The woman seated at the table, drawing the attention, was vaguely familiar. She wore her dark hair in luscious curls, and tossed it as she spoke, looking down her upturned nose at the people around the table.

"What happened then, Mandy?" Another woman asked, her hands clasped together in front of her stomach.

Mandy? Wait a second, isn't this Mandy Gilmore?

Gamma had mentioned her once before—Mandy was

a massive gossip in town. Why wasn't she staying at her house?

"What happened? Well, she ran off with her tail between her legs, of course. She'll soon learn not to cross me. Heaven knows, I always repay my debts."

"What, like a Lannister from *Game of Thrones*?" That had come from a taller woman with ginger curls.

"Shut up, Opal," Mandy replied. "You have no idea what we're talking about, and even if you did, you wouldn't have the intelligence to comprehend it."

The crowd let out various 'oofs' in response to that. The woman next to me clapped her hand over her mouth.

"You're all talk, Gilmore." Opal lifted a hand and yammered it at the other woman. "You act like you're a threat, but we know the truth around here."

"The truth?" Mandy leaned in, pressing her hands flat onto the tabletop, the crystal vase in the center rattling. "And what's that, Opal, darling? I'd love to hear it."

"That you're a failure. You sold your house, left Gossip with your head in the clouds, told everyone you were going to become a successful businesswoman, and now you're back. Back to scrape together the pieces of the life you have left."

"Witch!" Mandy scraped her chair back.

"All right, all right," I said, setting down the coffee pot

on the table. "That's enough, ladies. Everyone head back to their tables before things get out of hand."

Both Opal and Mandy stared daggers at me.

I flashed them both smiles. "We wouldn't want to ruin breakfast, would we? Lauren's prepared waffle cupcakes."

That distracted them. "Waffle cupcakes?" Opal's brow wrinkled. "How's that going to work?"

"Let's talk about it at your table." I grabbed my coffee pot and walked her away from Mandy. The crowd slowly dispersed, people muttering regret at having missed out on a show. The Gossip Inn was popular for its constant conflict.

If the rumors didn't start here then they weren't worth repeating. That was the mantra, anyway.

I seated Opal at her table, and she pursed her lips at me. "You shouldn't have interrupted. That woman needs a piece of my mind."

"We prefer peace of mind at the inn." I put up another of my best smiles.

Compared to what I'd been through in the past—hiding out from my rogue spy ex-husband and eventually helping put him behind bars when he found me—dealing with the guests was a cakewalk.

"What brings you to Gossip, Opal?" I asked.

"I live here," she replied, waspishly. "I'm staying here while they're fumigating my house. Roaches."

"Ah." I struggled not to grimace. Thankfully, my cell phone buzzed in the front pocket of my apron and distracted me. "Coffee?"

"I don't take caffeine." And she said it like I'd offered her an illegal substance too.

"Call me if you need anything." I hurried off before she could make good on that promise, bringing my phone out of my pocket.

I left the coffee pot on the sideboard, moving into the Gossip Inn's spacious foyer, the chandelier overhead off, but catching light in glimmers. The tables lining the hall were filled with trinkets from the days when the inn had been a museum—an eclectic collection of bits and bobs.

"This is Charlotte Smith," I answered the call—I would never get to use my true last name, Mission, again, but it was safer this way.

"Hello, Charlotte." A soft, rasping voice. "I've been trying to get through to you. I'm desperate."

"Who is this?"

"My name is Tina Rogers, and I need your help."

"My help."

"Yes," she said. "I understand that you have a certain set of skills. That you fix people's problems?"

"I do. But it depends on the problem and the price." I didn't have a set fee for helping people, but if it drew me away from the inn for long, I had to charge. I was technically a consultant now. Sort of like a P.I. without the fedora and coffee-stained shirt.

"My mother will handle your fee," Tina said. "I've asked her to text you about it, but I... I don't have long to talk. They're going to pull me off the phone soon."

"Who?"

"The police," she replied. "I'm calling you from the holding cell at the Gossip Police Station. I've been arrested on false charges, and I need you to help me prove my innocence."

"Miss Rogers, it's probably a better idea to invest in a lawyer." But I was tempted. It had been a long time since I'd felt useful.

"No! I'm not going to a lawyer. I'm going to make these idiots pay for ever having arrested me."

I took a breath. "OK. Before I accept your... case, I'll need to know what happened. You'll need to tell me everything." I glanced through the open doorway that led into the dining room. No one looked unhappy about the lack of service yet.

"I can't tell you everything now. I don't have much time."

"So give me the *CliffsNotes*."

"I was arrested for breaking into and vandalizing Josie Carlson's bakery, The Little Cake Shop. Apparently, they found my glove there—it was specially embroidered, you see—but it's not mine because—" The line went dead.

"Hello? Miss Rogers?" I pulled the cellphone away from my ear and frowned at the screen. "Darn."

My interest was piqued. A mystery case about a break-in that involved the local bakery? Which just so happened to be run by one of my least favorite people in Gossip?

And when I'd just started getting bored with the push and pull of everyday life at the inn?

Count me in.

Want to read more? You can grab **the first book** in *the Gossip Cozy Mystery series* on all major retailers.

Happy reading, friend!

9 781067 257163